EBONY OLSON

Cassidy

EBANDMUSE & PUBLICATIONS

Sydney, Australia

Ebony Olson

EBANDMUSE PUBLICATIONS

Published 2019

Published by
EbandMuse Publications
Sydney, Australia

ISBN-13: 978-0-6485000-2-5
Copyright © 2017 by **Ebony Olson.**

http://ebonyolson.com/

Dedication

To all my readers who reached out to ask for
this to be published.
To Kate who told me Holly's story couldn't end
with Henderson.
Thank you

Ebony Olson

Other Books Available by Ebony Olson

Hotel Series
Henderson
Cassidy
Holmes
Best Man

Black Mark Series
Black Mark's Resistance
Black Mark's Secret
Black Mark's Heart

Hierarch Series
Succumb
Numinous
Masked

Standalones
Of Shadow and Light

CHAPTER ONE

"You need to explain that rock on your finger," I demanded of Nichola, my eldest sister. She'd hidden it for most of the flight, but I managed to get a good look at it while she washed her hands in the bathroom.

"What rock?" Sadie asked sticking her face between us to take a gander. "Oh, my fucking God!"

"Sadie, you kiss your husband with that mouth?" Nichola chastised.

Sadie got a wicked glint in her eye. "My husband knows where my mouth has been; he doesn't care, as long as it's only kissing him these days."

"Back on subject. Where has your mouth been, that someone bought you this?"

Nichola blushed. "Holly, please." Raising a brow at her faux maiden behavior, I didn't give an inch. "Okay, fine," she snapped, a smile blooming on her face. "When I told Michael I was coming on a girls-only holiday, he got a bit possessive. He insisted on putting that on my finger. We'll announce the engagement when I get back."

"You're marrying your boss?" The sigh I emitted sounding only vaguely jealous.

Nodding energetically, Nichola pulled Sadie and me into a hug. "You two will have to be my bridesmaids again, so no getting pregnant anytime this year." Nichola looked at Sadie.

"What, is it my fault my husband enjoys this body?" Sadie ran her hands over her voluptuous figure. Despite three children and a small tummy she never used to have, the woman still had a killer body.

"Make him enjoy it with a piece of rubber between you," Nichola warned as we waited for our luggage.

"Now that's kinky." Sadie and I chuckled when Nichola froze and turned scarlet red with embarrassment.

Our luggage arrived, and we found the shuttle bus that would take us to our hotel. After exchanging several prompting looks with Nichola, Sadie turned to me, "So who was he?"

"Who was who?"

"Hello! The guy who broke your heart," Sadie opened her hands like it was an obvious question.

"What makes you think...?"

"Na-uh," Nichola cut me off. "You phone us out of the blue to announce you are taking leave and would we like to come on a holiday with you. You're our little sister, Holly, we know you. You taking a sudden trip out of town is code for, 'I broke up with the love of my life and can't bear to risk running into him'."

"Remember Max in high school?" Sadie patted my hand. "You two were hot and heavy. When he cheated on you, you jumped a bus to grandma's house faster than little red riding hood."

"Or your fiancé Claus at university?" Nichola added. "When you found out he had that fetish that made your stomach turn, you dumped him. Then you went on exchange for six months so you wouldn't have to see him at university every day."

"So, I ask again, darling little runaway sister," Sadie raised a brow. "Who was he?"

"Okay, let's start smaller." Nichola took pity on me. "How long were you together?"

"Not together, just screwing each other brainless for the last two years."

"Two years? Come on, Holly, that's more than just sex," Sadie considered me. "So, you were in a non-committed relationship?"

"No, we didn't see others, but we weren't dating or

anything either. Just an amazing quickie five days a week."

"How did you meet?" Nichola asked.

"We worked together." Knowing Nichola couldn't scold me for that now at least, I had no issue admitting it. "Actually, he was my boss."

"No fucking way!" Sadie looked ready to explode. "Tell me you weren't banging Benjamin Henderson?"

"Okay, I won't," I couldn't help laughing as both my sisters melted into a puddle of drool.

"So, fucking hot!" Sadie fanned herself. She met my eyes, "is he, you know, worth experiencing?"

"Sadie!" Nichola scolded.

"What? I'm married and have to live vicariously."

"He dumped her, give Holly a break," Nichola shoved Sadie's shoulder.

"Wait!" I looked at Nichola. "Why do you assume he dumped me?"

"Because it's Benjamin Henderson," Nichola 'duh'd' me. "Every girl wants to marry him; every girl gets their heart broken by him."

"I left him." Their jaws dropped open wide enough to showcase their tonsils. Sighing, I told them both the story. By the end of it, they were staring at me like I had two heads.

"You left Benjamin Henderson, the God of the sexy bachelors, waiting at his place, hard and ready for you?" Looking mortified, Sadie turned wide eyed to Nichola. "I've done three guys simultaneously, and am the queen of cum shots, and I'm speechless."

"A little louder, sis, the guys at the front of the bus haven't heard you're a You Tube cooking sensation." Rolling my eyes, I indicated the horrified faces of others on the bus near us.

Observing our surroundings, Sadie blew a kiss before turning back to Nichola. "Mum and dad were right about Holly."

"Really?"

Nodding in sympathy, a smirk pulling at the side of her

lips, Nichola patted my shoulder. "Afraid so, Holly."

Slumping down in my seat, I huffed. "Why did I invite you guys along again?"

They hugged me from either side. "Because we love you no matter how big a disappointment you are to the family."

After a few breaths, Sadie gave me a side look and lifted a brow. "You know, John has a cousin, freshly divorced, since you're into older men."

"Oh my god!" I threw them both off me. "I am not dating a politician, lawyer, or banker. I am not moving back home, and I am not being set up with any relative or friend of one of my sibling's partners."

Nichola shook her head with a chuckle. "Mum and dad were so right about you."

Groaning, I covered my face.

***

We finally arrived at the hotel, by lunchtime. We seemed to be the only three women not here with a partner or on their honeymoon. As soon as we alighted, it was something the valets, bellhop and concierge all paid attention too.

"Good afternoon, welcome to the Cassidy. My name is Henry and I'm the concierge. Do you have a reservation?"

"Yes, three rooms booked under Nichola Claire." Following the concierge to reception, he put us ahead of the line by using a spare terminal to check us in.

"I'm afraid only two of your reserved rooms are currently ready."

"Are they all the same room?" I asked. We could all go to one room for now if it meant a shower.

"Ah, yes, all deluxe rooms."

"Give my sisters the two available rooms; I can wait."

"Aren't you hungry?" Sadie asked surprised.

"Or dying for a shower?" Nichola queried.

"Aren't you?" I replied to both of them. "I can borrow one of your showers and then we can get some lunch before relaxing by the pool all afternoon?"

"If you check back with me after lunch, I'll let you know when your room is ready, Miss Claire."

After Nichola and Sadie checked in to their rooms, I went with Nichola to shower. Refreshed and dressed in a bikini with a sun dress over the top, I made my way back down to the lobby. While I waited for my sisters, I gathered pamphlets on tours, and places to eat.

"...will get that fixed up right away," a male voice assured a guest. The tall, gorgeous man caught my attention. Wearing the hotel uniform, he had sandy hair frosted by natural sun exposure. His caramel tan seemed more than likely natural, and his eyes were as blue as the ocean outside. He was Hawaii bottled into a man.

He turned from the receptionist he was helping and waved the concierge over. "Henry, why is room five-o-seven locked down? I need that room opened," the man asked the concierge as he passed the desk.

"Oh, the room is reserved, but wasn't ready for check-in. Once the cleaning crews finish, I need to find the guest and check her in," Henry explained.

"Well, it's clean, and I need it, so find the guest another room," the man decided, "unlock the room for me."

Henry moved closer to the desk. "Sean, that's the last deluxe room. If you take it, I'll need to upgrade the guest to a spa room for free. That's not good business."

Sean studied Henry. "How long is the guest staying for?"

Henry looked around a bit lost. "Four days." Both men looked at me surprised. "I'm staying four days, and, I'll take the free upgrade, thanks." My mischievous mind working. "For the inconvenience of giving my room away, and forcing me to wait longer, you can include breakfast."

Henry's mouth fell open a little; Sean was chewing the inside of his cheek. "How long is the wait on the spa room?" Sean asked the receptionist to his other side.

"Two hours," she replied after checking with housekeeping.

Sean exhaled, looked me over then turned to Henry. "Do it. Give her the upgrade and complimentary breakfast for the duration of her stay."

Sean called the shots, and worked during daylight; that made him the manager. Henry agreed, removed his hold on the now ready deluxe room and put a hold on the spa room. Sean instructed the receptionist he was standing next to, to check in the other couple.

"Ah, Sean, the spa room is only available two nights," Henry murmured, trying not to let me hear. I was pretending to read the pamphlet on volcano tours, but I'm pretty sure my lips twitched giving me away.

Sucking in a huge breath of annoyance, Sean moved over to Henry's computer. "Surely, you can find a room for the young lady, Henry."

"Currently, not without making her switch rooms halfway through her stay, I can't." Henry bit back politely, but with annoyance. Henry was searching through room by room to try and find one that was available.

"Oh, for the love of God!" Placing the pamphlets down as I stepped around the counter, I reached past a surprised Henry. Hitting the keyboard shortcut, I scanned the listings. "Here. Room seven fifteen is available for the next five days and is ready for check in. Will that suffice?" They both stared at me.

"That's a premier suite," Henry winced.

"Well, it suits me better than one of you sleeping on the couch so I could take the bed at your house, doesn't it?"

Sean raised a brow. I met the challenge with a smile. The side of Sean's mouth twitched. "Check our guest in, Henry," he directed.

Henry's eyes bulged. "Of course, Miss Claire, do you have your passport?" Sean waited long enough to catch my name, and then he headed off to deal with another problem.

Once I had my room key, I retrieved my bags from Nichola and stowed them in my room before we went to find food. After a very late lunch, we found three sun-beds by the pool, slathered on the sunscreen, and set ourselves up to rest. I took the sun bed in the shade; two years of night-shift does not give you a good UV tolerance.

Cassidy

Two hours later, Sadie stood up. "I'm going in for a dip," she declared and dived into the pool.

"I hate that she's had three kids and all it did was give her bigger boobs," Nichola grumbled to me.

"Mum kept her figure after having five kids."

"Mum is a politician's wife. It's eat like a rabbit or the media fat shames you," Nichola criticized.

We watched Sadie pull herself from the pool and Nichola scoffed. "I wish I had boobs like that."

As Sadie stood, a man walked up to her and whispered something in her ear before holding up his phone. Sadie smiled and shrugged and posed while the guy took a selfie with his tongue in her ear.

"Eww, I take it back, let her keep the tits," Nichola groaned in disgust.

"Is she famous?" I heard a woman ask her friend.

"Oh yeah, that's the You Tube chick who cooks and shit," her son answered.

It was like a bomb exploded. Everyone around us was trying to get a picture of themselves with Sadie. People started pushing and shoving each other. Sadie tried to calm them down, assuring they could get a group photo, but no one was listening.

"Shit," Nichola waded in, trying to help Sadie escape.

Looking around, I spied the lifeguard and waved him over. Once he was close enough, I signaled to use his whistle, which he did, as a fourth person fell into the pool.

"Everyone, your attention please." Pushing through the crowd with the lifeguard and another employee who had shown up. "Mrs. Fox is on holiday. But she will sign autographs and take selfies with polite fans who are willing to line up and take turns."

Grabbing Sadie's hand, I moved her away from the pool and over to a grassed area of the property. The other employee materialized a towel for Sadie. Everyone followed, forming a neat and polite line.

"As Mrs. Fox is doing this on her holiday, I hope you all respect there will only be one photo per person. Thank you."

Leaving Sadie there, I turned to talk to the employee. "Can you manage this?"

"You're not her manager?" He asked surprised.

"No," I scrunched my brow in disgust, "I'm her sister, and I'm on holiday too. These are your guests. Get your manager or concierge to come deal with this shit." Walking off, I joined Nichola back by the sun-bed.

"Should we dress and go sit by the bar and drink cocktails?" Nichola asked.

"Hell, yes!"

Pulling our sun-dresses on, we moved to the bar. Passing Sean, who was making his way toward the impromptu signing, his eyes locked onto me. Assessing each other as we passed, we both turned our heads to keep eye contact until we couldn't. Then I looked over my shoulder to admire his backside as he walked away.

"What was that?" Nichola asked with a smirk.

"The manager."

"Really? I was thinking rebound," Nichola cocked an eyebrow at me.

I laughed. "Jesus, I'd need a rebound to rebound from the rebound if I went there. He's a dish."

"Best served hot and hard," Nichola finished for me. We both started laughing as we got to the bar.

I'd missed my sisters.

CHAPTER TWO

My ideas book was where I wrote all the things I'd ever considered for when I finally became manager of a hotel. Every idea I'd ever instigated at Henderson was in this book. Even more that wasn't because they didn't suit the Henderson style of hotel.

It wasn't always for me. Some of my ideas were how I would improve the place at which I was staying. Things I would never actually pass on to the managers, but I liked to write it down. My dad always thought I'd end up a hotel reviewer, but tried to encourage me into law or medicine. He'd been happy when I'd chosen a business school after I'd finished my arts degree. He hadn't been happy I'd dumped my lawyer boyfriend and chosen to work in a hotel. We hadn't talked much after that.

"I'm calling it a night," Nichola slurred a little as she tried to stand up.

"Me too," Sadie laughed. "Too much sun and alcohol."

"I'm going to stay up a little longer. I'll see you at breakfast in the morning."

While my sisters leaned on each other to go inside the hotel, I took my book and walked down near the beach. We'd watched the sunset while we downed cocktails. Sighing as I leaned against a tree where the path met the beach, I watched the waves roll in in the dark. The spring breeze was lovely on my skin after the heat of the day.

Footsteps crunching down the path towards the beach cottages, broke the serenity. Deciding that was my cue to leave, I turned and started back up the path. My steps hesitated when I came face to face with Sean, the manager.

"Miss Claire," he greeted surprised. Looking around, he raised that sexy brow at me. "Lost your friends?"

"My sisters had a bit too much sun and cocktails and retired early." Brushing past him, I wondered if he knew how sexy that brow could be.

Sean's eyes noted the book I clutched to my chest. "Are you a writer?"

Adjusting my stance, I shifted the book behind me. "No, it's where I write my thoughts."

Sean's brows lifted. "You wander around with your diary?"

His brow popped up again, I laughed. "It's not like that either, no scandalous experiences or dear diary."

Sean smiled like he didn't believe me. He looked me over again. "So, Mrs. Fox, she's your biological sister?"

It wasn't the first-time people didn't believe it. None of us girls looked alike. "Yes, well, as far as our parents have told us. There are five of us, and all very different in appearance."

"So, you aren't in the same line of work as your sister?" Sean phrased the question with care.

"No, I'm afraid I'm not that good a cook," I laughed. Sean's smile dropped. His eyes flicked side to side, and brow grew heavy. "Oh, you mean...? No, and she doesn't do that anymore. Most of those people knew her for her cooking show, not her deep throat ability." Turning away while Sean still gaped at me for my openness, I took a step back up the path.

"Wait, you're angry?" Sean frowned at me.

Turning back around, I glared at him. "You insinuated I look like a porn actress. I'm allowed to be insulted. To clarify; I don't have an issue with my sister's former career. We all rebelled against our strict upbringing in our own way. Sadie was always comfortable in front of a camera, and she made a living from it. When she finished with it, she left with her dignity. There are actresses in Hollywood with their sex tapes who couldn't claim the same."

"I didn't mean..." Sean started. I raised a brow. He exhaled. "Okay, I was curious if the three of you were all taking a break from filming. Considering your age group, your sister's fame, and how hot all three of you are, it's a plausible conclusion."

He was right; I still wasn't flattered. "I'm five years younger than Sadie. When she became famous for fucking, I was still jail-bait." I enjoyed Sean's eyes bulging at my use of the F-word. "She finished with that world, married, and was pregnant with her first baby by the time I was legal. This is the first time anyone has ever implied my guilt by association. At least, it's the first time they had the balls to ask."

"Was that a compliment?" Sean chuckled.

Checking out his groin, I shrugged, then met his eyes again. "So that you know, my sister's lack of gag reflex isn't hereditary." Turning on my heel, I walked back to the hotel. I was in my room, running a bath when someone knocked at the door. "Who is it?"

"Room service," the female voice on the other side announced. Opening the door with care, my brows low with confusion. "Compliments of management." The woman smiled as she carried a tray in, placing it on the table for me. She handed me a small envelope on the way out. "Enjoy your evening, Miss Claire."

Closing the door after her, I opened the envelope to remove the business card. Embossed calligraphy showcased the name Sean Cassidy. Below his title of Hotel Manager, was his contact numbers and the Cassidy Hotel's emblem. On the back in a very neat script was handwriting.

I noticed you hadn't eaten dinner, so I saved you the best part. Please accept this as my apology for insulting you. Sean.

Lifting the lid exposed a banana crepe, smothered in Belgium chocolate. Smiling, I sat down to enjoy the gift. Once my sweet tooth was satisfied, I stripped and soaked in the tub big enough for two. Verging on sleep in the bath, I remembered sleeping there wasn't a safe option. Begrudgingly, I pulled the plug. Wrapping a towel around me before going to stand on the balcony, I looked out over the sea. It was a beautiful night.

Leaving the door open so I could listen to the waves, I removed the towel and crawled under the quilt naked. Reaching out, I turned off the light. The music of waves crashing to shore and the voices of nocturnal animals serenading me to sleep.

Knocking on my door disturbed a pleasant dream involving Belgium chocolate and nudity. "Who is it?"

"Room service, may I enter," a male voice called.

Remembering I negotiated breakfast, I didn't remember it being in the room. "Yes." I leaned up on my elbows to watch as the staff member carried a tray in and placed on the table. "I don't remember ordering breakfast," I told the attendant's back.

The staff member kept his back to me, which was good training. "For these rooms the in-room breakfast is complimentary, Miss Claire. Since you hadn't placed your order, Mr. Cassidy ordered for you."

"Should I ask?"

"Mr. Cassidy thought you were a bacon, eggs and waffles girl, I mean..."

"What kind of eggs?" I tried not to laugh at the attendant's faux pas.

"Scrambled, Miss Claire."

Smiling, I fell back into the bed. "Tell Mr. Cassidy he chose well, thank you." The attendant hesitated. Groaning, I pulled my quilt tight around me. "Wait, sorry, can you pass me my bag, I'm unable to go get it." The attendant located my bag, back-stepped to the bed and reached his arm back to me. "You can look, I've covered up."

The attendant, checked over his shoulder before he turned. Removing some notes, I handed them to him. He smiled and bowed his head. "Very generous, Miss Claire."

I laughed. "You earned it for not even trying to sneak a peek."

Cassidy

"There are things you can't unsee, Miss Claire." Realizing what he'd said, the attendant tried to back pedal. "Not that I'd want to unsee you, Miss Claire, just..."

"Settle," I waved his defense down. "I've been in the industry six years. I know what you meant. I'm forever scared."

Exhaling in relief, the attendant smiled. "My worst so far was an overweight man with more hair on his body than head."

"A month ago, I got punched out trying to save a prostitute getting strangled to death by her fat bastard of a client. Both of them were naked, but the woman barely survived. The son of a bitch trashed the room."

The attendant's eyes were huge. "You win."

"Damn straight I do, I didn't even tell you the worst part." Sinking down into the comfort of my bed, I closed my eyes. The attendant took the hint and left. I lay there for a moment, letting the sound of the ocean wash away all my thoughts of Hotel Henderson. With an audible sigh, I pulled on a robe and followed the smell of coffee to the table. Breakfast filled the hole in my stomach, and the freshly squeezed juice woke me up. It was still early, so there was no chance my sisters would be awake yet. Slipping into my swimmers, I went downstairs to the pool, and did forty minutes worth of laps.

Not long after I finished my shower and dressed for the day, I met my sisters for the shopping tour. After a morning shopping, we enjoyed lunch at the Cheesecake Factory. The afternoon consisted of more shopping, before returning to the hotel.

"Are you sure you don't want to do the climb with us?" Nichola checked as we made our ways back to our rooms.

"Volcanoes aren't my thing, especially not climbing back down at dusk. I would be the person to trip and break something," I excused.

"You still have your Dante's Peak phobia, don't you?" Sadie teased.

"Totally!" Ever since that movie, the idea of climbing a volcano gave me the willies. "Plus, I worry how my sulfur allergy might react being that close to the top of a volcano."

"God, remember how sick she got in Rotorua when the family went to New Zealand for that holiday?" Nichola reminded us. "You ended up hospitalized because you couldn't breathe."

"That was bad," Sadie agreed, "you definitely shouldn't risk it."

"Cocktails in the bar again tonight?" Nichola suggested instead. We chorused our agreement then parted ways to stash our shopping. Since the girls weren't big on water sports, I'd organized to do some surfing while they flew over the volcano. I'd done lessons while on holidays in my teens and was confident I could pick it back up.

Packing my bag with my notebook, towel, and brush, I made my way down to the beach. Three hours later, I rode my final wave ashore and returned the board. Happy I'd not only remembered how to surf, but I felt I'd improved on my skill a little.

Showering under the beach shower, I dried off and brushed my hair up into a ponytail. I didn't put my dress back on for the walk back up to the hotel. Everyone else walked around in their bikinis. Years of swimming and yoga made me comfortable enough to do the same.

"You're a bit red, could I get you some aloe?" The female staff member who was serving drinks by the pool offered as I passed.

"That would be nice, thank you. How much?"

"Complimentary. We don't like our guests getting burnt and not being able to enjoy their stay." She came back with a cocktail and a bottle of aloe. "Aloe Vera juice and coconut water to cool and hydrate the inside, and the gel for the outside. Would you like Paulo to do your back for you? He's a masseuse, so you can double up and get a massage at the same time."

It was a good on-sell. Paulo wouldn't be free, but I could do with a massage. "If Paulo is available, I'd love it."

Led to a tent with a massage table, I took a seat and enjoyed my juice. Paulo arrived a few minutes later. He was a native Hawaiian and, momentarily, his height, and thick arms terrified me. He explained his pricing structure and asked which I'd prefer. I decided to go with the full body rub down, all with the aloe. Paulo may have looked intimidating, but his hands were soft. He knew all the right places to release my muscles.

Thirty minutes later, I felt relaxed, hydrated, and tired. Not wanting to sleep, I put my dress on and pulled out my notebook to write. After noting down my positive and negative experiences during the day, I then wrote a few ideas I could take back to the Holmes City Resort with me. I probably should have sat down to write, but I worried I'd sleep, so I was walking around.

"Hmpf," a male grunted as I slammed into a solid object, my book and bag falling to the ground.

"God, I'm sorry," I apologized, certain that was my fault.

Turning to see who had walked into him, Sean blinked at me. "Miss Claire?" He bent and collected my stuff for me. "Did you want to talk to me?"

"No, I wasn't watching where I was walking." Seeing that Sean was reading my notebook, I took it back and shoved it into my bag. "Sorry, I was writing and walking, trying to stay awake, and zoned out," I tried to excuse my silliness. Sean kept quiet, his eyes appraising me. "I did want to thank you for dessert last night, and breakfast this morning, I didn't realize how hungry I was."

Sean raised that eyebrow as someone behind him cacked themselves laughing. Forehead slapping myself, when I heard what I said, I tried again. "That came out wrong," I apologized again.

Sean's smile grew. "I'm glad you were satisfied," he teased, making me blush. Sean looked around. "I see you have lost your sisters again?"

"They are doing the sunset volcano tour."

"You didn't join them?" Sean moved us out of the way of his staff who were trying to get stuff done.

Removing my arm from his gentle grasp, I stepped another step away. "I don't do volcanoes. I went surfing instead."

"I thought the lessons ran in the morning?"

"They do, I didn't need lessons. I learned to surf years ago."

Sean smiled. "So, you are alone for dinner?"

"I am."

Sean turned around to one of the staff. "Gus, tell the others I'm taking my dinner break."

There was a murmur of affirmation behind him, then Sean placed his hand in the small of my back. "Come, Miss Claire, let's get you fed so you can get to bed early."

I laughed. "I'm meeting my sisters for cocktails when they get back, so I doubt that will happen."

Sean turned to meet my eyes, smile lines surrounding his humored blues. "Why didn't you take an afternoon nap then?"

"I was fine till I got the massage from Paulo. After that, the sun and surf caught up with me."

Sean looked ahead. "Paulo is very skilled with his hands."

"Every woman loves a man who is good with his hands," I responded with a cheeky smile. Sean's mouth twitch, but he didn't take the bait.

We stepped down into the Grotto restaurant. It was a beautiful rock pool haven that looked out over the beach and the sunset. "Table for two please, Monica," Sean greeted the hostess.

Monica grabbed two menus and led us to our table, which happened to be one of the best tables in the place. I guess Sean was the boss. We sat and browsed the menus, placed our orders, and then I watched the sun kiss the horizon. "Do you live here?" I sighed, mesmerized by the perfect sunset.

"The furthest beach villa is mine," Sean answered. I could feel his eyes on me.

"Must be nice to enjoy this daily."

"I admit, I still enjoy it after a decade. I work through it five days a week, so it still holds its beauty on the weekends for me," Sean answered. "You don't live near the beach I take it?"

"My apartment overlooks park lands, but I work and live in the city. I usually work weekends and miss the sunrise and sunset."

"You would have missed it tonight if you hadn't walked into me, correct?" Sean queried.

"I guess so." Considering how much I loved the sunset and sunrise, but rarely had time to see it, I frowned. Taking out my notebook, I jotted a note down. A simulated sunrise and sunset were a fantastic idea for business travelers.

"Miss Claire?" Looking up at Sean's coaxing, I saw him eying my notebook. "Put the book away. Stop working, and enjoy the sunset."

Embarrassment heated my cheeks. Closing my book, I slipped it back into my bag as our drinks arrived. Sipping my coconut water with pineapple juice, I watched the sun sink into the ocean. "I should have stayed longer," I sighed as night descended.

"Than four nights?"

"I only have three more sunsets before I jump the boat home."

"You're cruising back to Australia?" Sean asked surprised.

"Yes, a friend suggested it. I had a month. I should have stayed longer and caught a later ship."

"No boyfriend who would miss you?" Sean asked, failing to be casual about it.

A stone set in my stomach. I'd thought about Benjamin a lot, but I was trying not to. "No. I haven't had one of those in a long time," I admitted. "I've focused on my career since I left university and not had time for dating."

"No one has time for dating unless they make time," Sean lectured.

"I was seeing someone, but it wasn't serious, and we decided that needed to end."

"Wasn't serious for him or you?" Sean queried, seeming to see right through me.

"Either of us," I defended, "but I did think I meant more than it turned out."

Sean's eyes flicked over me then sat back as a waiter

served our meals. He waited till the wait staff left. "Ten years ago, I came here on holiday with my girlfriend. A week after we got home to San Francisco, the lawyer she was also seeing proposed, and she left me. Everything reminded me of her and her cheating. I thought of the last place I was happy. I jumped on a plane and came here. Strange as it was, we barely spent any time together here, since we had different interests. So, this place didn't make me think of her. I stayed."

"Has there been anyone since?"

"I've dated, but nothing serious."

"Holiday flings?"

"Usually no, I rarely fraternize with guests," Sean negated my insinuation.

"Yet, you are having dinner with me?"

"Oh, this is business, Miss Claire. I worried you'd forget to eat again."

I smirked as I lifted my drink. "Well, here's to two people working and eating."

Sean raised a brow. "I thought you were on holiday, Miss Claire?"

Winking at him, I drank a sip of my hydration in a glass.

CHAPTER THREE

"...took a million photos. I'll have some decent ones in there somewhere," Sadie chattered.

We were two hours into cocktails, which translated to giggly and sarcastic. Nichola and Sadie were both sun-burnt. Tomorrow, Sadie would be brown, and Nichola would have freckles for the first time in years. After an afternoon of hydrating, I was a blush pink. I'd alternated real cocktails with nonalcoholic hydration cocktails.

"You ladies look to be having fun. Could I interest one of you in a dance?" A man somewhere around Nichola's age, who could have been attractive if his own ego wasn't in the way, inquired.

"I so would, but I'm married," Sadie flashed her ring.

"Same, but engaged," Nichola waved her ring.

The guy looked to me waiting. "Yeah, same, if I was even remotely interested, but I'm not." The guy smiled ready to move on, then actually heard what I said. You could see it on his face, trying to figure out if he'd heard me right.

Nichola and Sadie were wetting themselves trying not to laugh in the guy's face. He walked away still confused. "Jesus, you're mean," Nichola laughed. "That's the fifth guy you've sent off checking if his balls are still intact tonight, and he wasn't half bad."

"Which half? Were we looking at opposite ends?"

"You were," Sadie assured. "You were looking at his head, Nichola was looking at his balls. That's how she noticed they'd shriveled up."

We all started laughing again. "Ladies, enjoying your evening?" Sean approached us from the staff side of the bar.

"Are you working a double shift?" I asked with a raised brow.

"Covering so Daniel could have his break," Sean smiled. "I'll be finishing as soon as he comes back."

I didn't realize I was sitting there smiling at Sean till Nichola nudged me. "You going to introduce us, Holly?"

"Sean is the Manager of this fine establishment," I offered. "My sisters, Nichola, and Sadie."

"A pleasure," Sean smiled. "Refills?"

The girls ordered cocktails with the usual suggestive names. Sean laughed looking to me. "Guess?" I teased.

"That's dangerous," Sean teased back. "What about a Mountain Dew Me?"

Nichola had to cover her mouth to stop from spitting her drink on the bar. "Honey, with Holly, you'd have to give her a Leg Spreader before you'd ever get anywhere with her," Sadie laughed.

"Really?" Sean lifted a brow at me.

"Or a Rowie," Nichola smiled. "I'm pretty sure that's what..."

"Say his name, and I swear you'll never see the sunrise," I warned.

"…got her drinking for her to let him take the big V," Nichola finished.

"I was sober losing my virginity," I assured Sean. "Possibly not when I said yes to the perv's marriage proposal, but definitely for that." My sisters kept laughing. Meeting Sean's eyes, I lifted my brow in challenge. "Surprise me. Let's see if you get this right?"

Sean grinned and started mixing. He served Nichola and Sadie first before mixing my drink. It was Friday night. Most of the young people had gone into town to go clubbing. The rest of the resort seemed to be heading to bed. Sean placed a pink drink in front of me. Taking a sip, I let the smooth delight coating my tongue light up my eyes.

"What does it taste like?" Sean asked.

Cassidy

My sisters hooted as I stood, grabbed his shirt to pull him forward across the bar and French kissed him. Happily surprised, Sean didn't pull away. Unlike when Daniel asked Nichola that question, I didn't pull away either.

When we parted, Sean licked his lips, his pupils dilated. "That was pretty nice," he murmured.

"What's it called?" I smiled, knowing he wasn't referring to the drink.

"Usually, Angel's Slit, but I'm renaming it Angel's kiss for tonight."

"Finally," Sadie patted me on the back, "well done, Holly." Sadie looked to Nichola. "Holly wins!"

Sean frowned when I threw my hands in the air. "I've walked into a bet, haven't I?"

"A dare," I corrected. "Winner got to choose tomorrow afternoons activity, and now it's snorkeling."

My sisters groaned in unison. "Come off it, Holly. You know we hate water sports," Sadie whined.

"Why don't I take you snorkeling, and you let your sisters do something you don't like to do?" Sean offered.

"Awesome idea," Sadie declared standing up. "You two should organize that now, while Nichola and I call it a night. See you in the morning."

Sadie and Nichola ran off, holding hands and giggling as they looked over their shoulders at us. I rolled my eyes. Sean chuckled. "Your sisters aren't subtle."

"No, but they are drunk enough to think they are," I smiled drinking the rest of my cocktail. "So, snorkeling?"

"Snorkeling." We sat there looking at each other until someone further around the bar cleared their throat. "Excuse me," Sean smiled then went to serve the man and his friend.

Finishing my drink, I stood up. The world was a little unstable. I sat back down. "You okay?" Sean asked coming back over.

"What was in that drink?" I tried to get the world to stabilize. "And why am I so hot?"

"Yeah, I should have explained where the drink got its name."

"Sean, I'm back," Daniel walked back in behind the bar, "thanks for covering."

"Not a problem," Sean called walking around and collecting my arm. "You're not a big drinker, are you?"

"Not really." Sean helped me back inside towards the elevators. "That last one kicked my arse." I stumbled as we stepped into the elevator, Sean reached out to catch me and ended up hugging me. "You smell delicious," I murmured breathing him in.

"Thank you, but that might be the drink talking," Sean informed me, setting me back on my feet. "There is an ingredient in that drink called Cupid's dart. It gives the drink that smooth texture on the tongue which is supposed to feel like a woman's..." Sean cleared his throat. "Anyway, this ingredient can cause an unusual allergic reaction. I guess you're one of the five percent of the world allergic to it," Sean cringed.

"In what way?" I asked, leaning in to get another whiff of him.

"It can be a very powerful aphrodisiac for those allergic." Sean's eyes transfixed on one of my legs.

Looking down, I realized I'd started running my hand up my thigh and lifted my sun-dress with it. I wanted to smack myself. Instead, I took Sean's hand and moved it to my thigh instead. "God, that feels good," I moaned.

"Holly, I don't sleep with my customers." Sean's hand reached the junction between my thighs.

"Okay, don't sleep with me," I murmured. It was like I was locked out of the control-room of my body while my doppelgänger took over. I'd think one thing, the right thing, and do exactly the fucking opposite. "Sean, help me." I meant for him to help me take back control, but the doppelgänger slipped his hand down the front of my knickers.

Sean's fingers immediately found my already swollen and tender clit. "Fuck, I should have taken you to my place." Sean was tapping out the distress signal in Morse code on my clit. Moaning, I gripped his wrist like it was my lifeline.

Cassidy

The elevator arrived at my floor. Sean stole his hand back just before the door opened and one of his staff smiled at him. "Everything okay, Sean?"

Forcing a smile, Sean nodded. "Miss Claire is reacting to something she drank and needs help getting to her room. Would you mind taking over for me? My shift finished an hour ago."

I could have kissed Sean at that moment for palming me off to a female staff member. The doppelgänger agreeing with that idea, stepped forward. Sean saved us both by turning me to the female. She caught me and frowned. "Does she need a doctor?"

"Just her bed will be enough, Deidre," Sean assured as Deidre helped me stumble down the corridor.

The elevator doors shut. I sighed with relief. "Thank you."

With no bisexual tendencies at all, this woman was not fueling my fire. She got me to my room and helped me inside. "Can I get you anything?"

Your bosses hand back on my... "I'm good, thank you." Crawling onto my bed with a groan, I fell face down. My arm pinned under me, so my fingers were already pressing my swollen bud.

"I hope you feel better in the morning," Deidre offered. "If you need anything please call."

Whimpering a thank you, I bit lip while my fingers pinched my clit. Giving me a sympathetic look, Deidre left. Lying there for several minutes, my climax tightrope walked the edge. I needed a guy to be doing this. I needed Benjamin. Tears filled my eyes remembering him. No, that wasn't going to work.

Reaching over to the bedside table, I grabbed Sean's business card. Picking up the phone, I called his mobile. "Sean Cassidy speaking."

"You need to talk dirty to me."

"Excuse me?"

"You gave me the damn drink, and I can't get off. Talk dirty to me."

"Holly?" Sean sounded surprised. "Shit, give me a

minute."

My body reacted to his voice. "Actually, screw talking dirty; just talk. You have the deepest voice I've ever heard. It's a fucking turn on to hear it."

"You know you kissed me, right?" Sean reminded me. "I can't remember the last time someone kissed me like that."

"I love kissing, and you are a very good kisser," I breathed. "I wish you were kissing me right now."

"Only kissing you?"

"I didn't say where I wish you were kissing me," I wheezed. Oh god, the idea of Sean's tongue flicking my bean. "Fuck!" I panted, and came. I came harder than I ever had masturbating before, and probably more than I had during sex. Lying there getting my breathing under control, I felt so, very, relaxed.

Turning my head, ready to fall asleep, I saw the phone. Picking it up, I put it to my ear. "Sean?"

"Oh good, I worried you'd passed out," Sean teased.

"I'm about to. Sean?"

"Don't worry, Holly, I won't mention this ever happened."

"I was going to ask for some of that stuff," I murmured, half asleep. "That's the best orgasm I've ever had."

Sean was quiet for a minute. "Meet me by the jetty at one tomorrow afternoon. Goodnight, Holly."

Stretching to put the phone back in its cradle, I didn't stay awake long enough to know if I hung it up.

CHAPTER FOUR

You know the worst part about not being drunk when you do shit? Remembering when you wake up. When room service arrived in the morning, I woke up feeling happy and tingly. Still dressed from yesterday, I could tip the staff member myself. It wasn't until I noticed the phone on the floor that I picked it up and wondered why it was there. That's when the elevator, the phone call, and that amazing orgasm, all came flooding back. Embarrassed didn't cover it. Mortified seemed a more suitable adjective.

Meeting my sisters for the tour to Pearl Harbor, I tried very hard not to remember those details. "Are you still snorkeling with Sean this afternoon?" Nichola prodded as we explored.

"At one."

"Did anything happen after we left last night?" Sadie shoulder bumped me from the other side.

"I went to bed, alone." I added the last to prevent any further investigation.

"Bugger," Nichola sighed, "I was sure he was into you."

Sadie agreed. "You should bang that guy, Holly, and tell us all about it."

"Should I ask why?"

"Because, Sadie's married, and I'm all but. "Since we can't shag that beautiful specimen, it all falls to you to enjoy what God created for women to enjoy."

"He might have a pin dick."

"With a voice that deep," Sadie laughed, "not a chance."

"He could be a selfish lay?"

"You are making excuses," Nichola scolded. "What's holding you back, Holly? You're single, hot, young. You are everything a guy like him wants for a few nights of fun. Get on it already and forget Benjamin Henderson ever existed."

"Oh my god!" I yelled. "This isn't going to happen. I'm not the sort of girl who meets a guy and jumps into bed with him. I don't do one-night stands or holiday fuck frenzies."

There was a static quiet all around us. Around us were either amused or appalled faces of other tourists. Was there a shade of embarrassment brighter than red?

"I'm sorry. Sisters, you know." Gesturing to my laughing sisters. Throwing my hands up in frustration, I stormed off. These sorts of walk around, touch nothing, sightseeing tours, never enthused me much. Only if it came with role-playing and popcorn.

When it came time to head back to the hotel, Nichola put her arm around my waist and rested her head against mine. "We care about you, Holly. If it's too soon, or too much, we understand."

"Because mum and dad were so right about you," Sadie teased.

Sighing, I looked at the two guys my age checking out a teenage girl. "See the blond to my left?" They looked at me, then Sadie and nodded. "Isn't she that porn star? Fox something?" Walking off, I let that play out.

"Holy shit, that's Fox Nastee!" one of them exclaimed. Sadie spent the bus ride with the two guys hitting on her and nearly taking it to the point of assault.

"You're evil when you're angry," Nichola murmured. "I saw you tell those boys who she was."

"Don't know what you mean," I responded, staring out the window.

An hour later I was sitting on the jetty waiting for Sean. "Good afternoon," he smiled down at me. Standing up, I brushed off my bottom. Sean assessed me. "Not a good afternoon?"

"Sisters spent the morning giving me a hard time about

my life choices."

"Isn't that what siblings do?"

"I've been coping it from my parents and siblings all my life. There was a huge age difference when I was younger, so you expect it." I stepped towards him. "But, when one sister's perfect marriage ended up a front-page scandal. The other was infamous enough in the porn world that people still recognize her. You'd think that would give you a bit of acceptance." Sean just watched me. "I'm sorry, that was a bit of a rant."

"Actually, I'm wondering what you've done to still be at the bottom of the pecking order. Did you kill someone?"

"No."

"Drug addict?"

"I've never even smoked."

"Lesbian?"

"Deidre would be smiling this morning if I was even bi-curious," I teased.

Sean smirked, tried to swallow it and looked to the side. He'd promised never to mention last night. "We should get going." Nodding, I followed him out to the end of the jetty.

Opening a storage box, Sean removed the gear we'd need. Moving to the preparation point he pulled his shirt over his head. I stared. I mean, it was worth looking. He was no Benjamin with his gym, swim, run body, but Sean was the outdoors and active type.

"Something wrong?" Sean asked, frowning when I was just standing there.

"I was wondering how old you are?" Covering my perving, I moved forward to get myself ready.

"Thirty-five, is it important?"

"No, I picked you to be around Sadie's age. Just wasn't sure if I was right." Lifting my skater dress over my head to leave me in my bikini.

There was no response from Sean. When I turned, he blinked and looked away. "How old are you?" Sean countered.

"Twenty-eight."

"You look younger." Sean's eyes went to my boobs.

"Night shift causes limited sun exposure."

"Night shift? And you work weekends? According to the rumor amongst my staff, you work in the industry." Sean considered me as he handed me my flippers. "Are you a concierge?"

"I was, many years ago now. I've been working my way up for the past six years."

"Are you a hotel manager?"

"I was assistant manager till recently." My humor fading. Sean gave me that questioning look. "I was sexually harassed by a senior manager. When I reported it, the owner accused me of making it up because I wanted the manager's job. I had five years of leave accrued. I cashed it in, then handed in my resignation as I walked out the door."

Sean frowned and looked down at his feet. "So, you're between jobs?"

"No, I have a new job, but one dealing with only the staff instead of the clients now." I didn't want him worrying I was looking for his job here. I mean, he owns the place, his job is pretty safe. "Should we get some snorkeling done?" Picking up my mask, I walked to the jump point.

"You've done this before?" Sean asked as he came up beside me.

I set my mask in place. "Try and keep up," I teased, held my mask and jumped in.

Sean jumped in while I was airing my snorkel, then I led the way to the reef. We were down there for a while, enjoying the fish and colors. This side of the resort, the reef protected the beach, so it's where all the calm water activities occurred. The other side of the peninsula on which the Cassidy sat, was the true beach. The waves were good for surfing, and windsurfing. It was a great set up here.

Sean tapped me on the shoulder and gestured time to go back. Following him in, he helped me back up onto the jetty. We packed up quietly, drying ourselves with our towels before we walked towards land. "I'm this way," Sean gestured along the beach when we stepped off the jetty.

"Thank you, for taking me out. It was very kind of you."

"Well, I usually spend my weekends enjoying the islands, so it was my pleasure." Smiling, I went to walk back to the hotel. "Holly, would you like to have dinner with me tonight? There's this place, best sunset on the entire island."

"How can I turn down another amazing sunset?"

That made Sean grin. "Be ready in an hour. I'll meet you back here." Sean dashed away before I could question the meeting point. When I thought about it, he probably didn't want his staff to think he was fraternizing with a guest.

Back in my room, I showered and changed into a more anything-goes dress. Grabbing my cardigan and my bag, I headed back down the beach. Stopping for an aloe juice on the way, to help with hydration.

Sean was waiting on the jetty when I arrived. Smiling at me, he took my hand, walking me up the jetty to one of the small boats moored there. I didn't question it when he led me on board, untied the rope, and cruised us out and around the next peninsula.

Sean ran the boat ashore on a smaller beach which only had a forest. Collecting a hamper, Sean helped me climb forward to jump down onto the sand. Walking into the forest, then up some stone steps, we emerged on top of a cliff. We were above all the trees, able to look out to sea unhindered.

Setting down the hamper Sean unpacked it before taking a seat. "Let's eat," he encouraged. By the looks of it, the food was from the hotel kitchen. We sat and enjoyed still warm canapés, water, and mini cheesecakes for dessert. Sean brought wine, but when I decline after so much sun, Sean put the bottle away and poured water for both of us. We ate our entire meal in a comfortable silence, watching the sun sink below the horizon.

Before the light left us entirely, Sean packed up the hamper, pulled out a torch, and led the way back to the boat. When we got back to the jetty, he walked me up to the resort in silence. We'd barely said a word to each other the entire night.

Fare welling me in the lobby with a simple goodnight, Sean left the hamper with the front desk before he left. Yeah, the staff took note, but he hadn't kissed me or touch me, so it was something to intrigue them right now.

Up in my room and unable to sleep, I wandered out onto the balcony. I stood staring at the waves for a while before I wondered why I was doing it from such a disconnected location.

Making my way down to the beach, I drifted aimlessly, enjoying the night and the peace. Finding a spot where the moon shone across the water perfectly, I stood there staring out. It had to be the most beautiful place on this side of the peninsula.

"I'll listen and not judge if you want to talk about it," Sean offered as he came to stand next to me. He stood beside me shirtless, a pair of cargo shorts hanging on his hips like he'd pulled them on in a hurry.

"Where did you come from?" Sean pointed out a dim light. I made out the silhouette of one of the beach cottages, the last one along this stretch of beach. It was set a bit apart from the others, nestled a bit deeper into the trees. "You've got the best view of the beach."

"I had my cottage built for this view, and a bit of privacy."

Sitting on the sand, I looked out over the water. "My father's a respected politician back home. We grew up around other prominent political families. When I was fourteen, I started dating the then Prime Minister's son. We were together for two years. It ended when I found out he'd slept with another girl." Fidgeting with the hem of my dress, still feeling a piece of that insecure teenager within me.

"The break up was quiet. I didn't even tell my parents. But the media used to make a big thing about us dating because our parents were opposing parties. So, when it became obvious, we'd broken up, the media sniffed out the reason. One Sunday I woke to my name and the words 'dumped for staying a virgin', scrawled across the front page."

Sean remained quiet.

"The article revealed I'd refused to have sex, so he went

elsewhere, and when I found out, he dumped me. My parents were angry at me. It was like I'd disappointed them for not giving into the pressure to have sex before I was ready. I was only sixteen. It got worse. Another paper placed pictures of Sadie and I side by side, the words, 'Exact Opposites' above it. They labeled me frigid, uptight, and various other nasty terms for respecting myself. I hated it. I wrote a letter to a better media outlet expressing my disappointment. In the media, in my parent's reaction, and in the prime minister's son for even talking about it. It got printed. I received a barrage of support from the public. My parents grounded me."

"That's a hard line to tow," Sean murmured.

"I decided that I didn't agree with my parent's values and chose to do an arts degree at university. My father was not happy. When I started dating a charming law student, my family acted like I was a lost child finally found. After we got engaged, my fiancé told me particular expectations of me as his future wife. Things that I was not down with doing. So, I ended the relationship. You can imagine how that went down."

"So, your acceptance with your parents revolves around the men you date? So why were your sisters paying you out about the past?"

"Oh, they weren't. It's..." I sighed. "When all the stuff in the media happened with the Prime Minister's son, I ran away to my grandmother's. My parents can't stand her. She sort of marches to her own tune. When they finally found me, both my parents yelled some stuff at me. My grandmother and my brothers and sisters heard everything. It gutted me, but for my siblings, it was water off a duck's back. They make fun of me now by referring to it. They say, 'Mum and dad were right about you', whenever I do something with which they don't agree. I know they are just taking the piss, but..."

"It reminds you how you've never been good enough?" Sean finished for me.

"Yeah." Standing up, I walked down to the water's edge.

"After I broke off my engagement, I moved to Sydney to live my own life, dance to my own tune. I've never gone home again. Not for Christmas or anything," I confessed. "Last year, there was a big event on, my family were all together in the papers. Mr. and Mrs. Claire and their four children."

Moving up next to me, Sean took my hand. "Come on." He tugged me after him.

"Where are we going?" I asked as we walked back up the beach.

Sean looked back at me and winked.

CHAPTER FIVE

His cottage, that's where he took me. Into his inner sanctum where he insisted I sit on the lounge while he cooked up popcorn. "If you plan to do something kinky with that popcorn, I need to warn you that kink isn't my thing," I called into the kitchen.

Smirking at me, Sean pulled two bottles of soda out of the fridge. Opening them as he walked back into the lounge room, Sean placed one in front of me. "I told you, I don't fraternize with guests."

"I'm in your place," I pointed out, "this constitutes fraternizing."

Leaning down, Sean placed his hand on the couch behind me. "That's not fraternizing to me." His other hand dropped and trailed his cold bottle up my inner thigh, pushing my dress up.

"Sean!" Biting my lip, I grabbed his wrist to stop his progress.

"That was me fraternizing." Sean smiled before standing back up straight. "So, we're clear." He winked at me, lifted his drink to his mouth, and went back to the kitchen.

Grabbing my bottle, I drank from it. I needed to cool down because Sean half naked and teasing was a hell of a sensory experience. Coming back out with the popcorn, Sean dropped into the seat next to me on the lounge, and held the popcorn out to me. Taking it into my lap I grabbed a few while he picked up the remote.

"Okay, nothing romantic, no sob stories..."

"No horror," I jibbed in.

Sean smirked. "Thrillers it is." Opening the Netflix page, Sean scanned through till he found a movie he wanted to watch and pressed play. He got up long enough to turn off the light before sitting back down.

Placing the popcorn between us, we both sank into the lounge watching the movie. After it finished, came another movie. It was a bit slower, and half-way through, I felt myself dozing. I turned to get comfortable and found Sean's shoulder. His arm wrapped around me and pulled me into him. I fell asleep.

I woke up in the middle of the night with my cheek resting on Sean's chest. He was lying on the lounge with me squeezed between his body and the back rest. When I tried to get up without waking him, Sean's arm tightened around my waist. "Stay, it's late."

"I should go." Sean released me. Managing to climb off him without falling and hurting either of us, I dropped a kiss to Sean's cheek. "Thank you for listening."

Sean grabbed my hand. "Spend the day with me?" His eyes slit enough to watch me.

"It's my last day..."

"I know, spend it with me?"

Considering him, I smiled. "We both need some more sleep first."

Groaning, Sean stood up, gave me a tired smile, and led me into his bedroom. He crawled onto his bed before turning to look at me, his hand gripping mine to force me to follow. I stared at the bed amazed. "Sean, I haven't shared a bed with anyone in eight years."

Sean tugged me down causing me to stumble forward into his arms. "Ten years for me. Go to sleep, Holly." Dismissing my worry, Sean fell straight back to sleep.

Smirking at how cute he was, I snuggled into him and drifted back to sleep as well. The next time I woke, I was alone. The sun was up, the scent of yummy food, like bacon and pancakes, and syrup filling the cottage. Scrambling out of bed to use the bathroom, I made myself decent before moving out to the open plan living area.

Sean was in the kitchen, still in only his cargo pants, but with the addition of an apron. When he turned and saw me approach, his smile lit up the room. "Good morning. I hope you're hungry?"

"I'm ravenous." Stalking toward the kitchen bench, I eyed the two plates of food. "Can I help?"

"Pour two glasses of juice and grab some cutlery for the table," Sean suggested.

Following his direction, I then stood in the dining room taking in his place in daylight. It was neat and tidy but still lived in. There were photos of himself with a man who, by the similarity, had to be his dad on a bookshelf. Lifting the one from his graduation day to get a better look, I noticed a framed certificate behind it. A combined law and business degree certificate.

Swallowing the sudden ball of distaste in my mouth, I put the photo back. On the shelves below stood science fiction novels, adventure magazines, and cookbooks. He had more cookbooks than Mitchell, my yoga instructor. For a moment, I considered the option Sean was gay. Then I remembered the way he kissed me back at the bar two nights ago, and dismissed it.

"Come and eat," Sean whispered in my ear. Jumping, I spun, slamming back into the bookshelf. "Shit, are you okay?" Sean grasped my arms, just as wide-eyed as I was.

"Yes, sorry, I was lost in thought and you startled me."

"Really? I hadn't noticed." Sean physically moved me to the table and my seat. "Eat, ravenous one." Then took his seat.

We ate quietly for several minutes. I wasn't lying about being hungry, and the food was delicious. "Are you going to ask, or do you want me to pretend you didn't see my degree?" Sean eventually prompted.

"You sat the bar?"

"I did. I passed with flying colors."

"When you spoke about your ex, the way you spat his occupation, I wouldn't have considered you were one."

"That's because I'm not," Sean clarified. "I majored in corporate law. I interned, sat the bar, and had a starting position in a prominent law firm. Yet, I left it all behind a month after the woman I loved left me for a criminal attorney. He also happened to be my older brother."

My knife and fork froze in mid-air. Sean watched me. Picking up my juice, I took a sip. "You only have photos of your father?"

"My mother died when I was six months old; my father raised us both himself. With nannies of course, but still, he was there a lot," Sean revealed.

"He's a lawyer too?"

Sean's fingers gripped his cutlery. "He was. He gave it up to pursue other interests."

Recognizing a shut down when I saw one, I changed direction. Dad's work was a no-go topic. "Most of those photos are here, so he comes to visit?"

Sean relaxed a little, sympathy filling his eyes. "Yes. My father wasn't happy at first, but he could see how much happier I was here and supported my career change."

"Do you see your brother?"

"At family gatherings."

"Are they still together?"

Sean smirked. "Unhappily so." We met each other's eyes. Sean started laughing. "Okay, so he saved me from a bad marriage, but he was still my brother, and he was sleeping with my long-term girlfriend."

"I don't disagree with that sentiment," I shrugged, letting him know I didn't think he was a bad person.

Sean sat back. "You mentioned you were in a long-term casual thing?" I lifted my eyes to his. "Why did you do that when you are a person who doesn't do casual?"

"What makes you think I don't do casual?" I tried to avoid answering.

"A decade worth of experience of women trying to get in my pants, And, the fact that you announced it at Pearl Harbor to everyone on tour," Sean smirked.

My cheeks flushed with heat. "You heard about that?"

Cassidy

"Some of the other guests were discussing it on their return. That and the presence of a porn star in the hotel."

"You need to wipe that grin off your face," I warned him. "You knew why I was upset before you came down to go snorkeling, didn't you?"

"I knew you'd gotten upset; I didn't know to what extent."

I stood up. "Thanks for breakfast. I should go shower and change," I excused. I headed for the door to the path. "Anything specific I need for today?"

"Swimmers, a hat, sunscreen, and a smile," Sean informed me.

"Okay, I'll be back in an hour."

"Meet me in the lobby." Standing up, Sean took our plates to his sink and started cleaning up.

Nodding, I went back to the hotel. In my room, I stood in the shower considering my options. I had many. Sean was right. I'd been very upset last night over something so far in my past it shouldn't matter anymore. So why did it?

Back downstairs, I ran into Nichola in the lobby. "There you are, is everything alright?"

"Yes, I'm about to head out for the day," I explained.

Nichola frowned at me. She looked at my shorts and singlet over my bikini. "More water sports," she decided. "I don't know how you haven't burnt yourself with all your time in the water the last few days?"

"Lots of hydration and sunscreen."

"Well, Sadie and I are going on a horseback tour. Are you sure you don't want to join us?" Nichola checked.

Smiling, I kissed her cheek as I saw Sean enter the lobby. "I'm very sure. Have fun."

Moving away from her to meet Sean. "Everything okay?" He checked.

"Sure, let's go." Smiling, I let him lead the way. Peering over my shoulder at Nichola; she was smiling like a Cheshire watching me leave with Sean. Oh, if only my family knew.

CHAPTER SIX

It started in a helicopter. Not only did Sean take me on the aerial tour of the island, but he flew the helicopter himself. "I like to be in control," Sean confessed. Taking the stick in his hands, he lifted us off the helipad. Flying the route of the usual tour, he then showed me a few of his favorite sights.

Next, we went paddle boarding. Then it was lunch from Sean's favorite food outlet. In the afternoon, we went horseback riding. Not the trail rides my sisters had gone on in the morning, but a more intimate trail.

Sean saddled his horse himself, before helping me onto another horse. "This isn't part of the normal tour," Sean revealed as he led me down a steep path.

"I'm glad, or your insurance would be a killer." The track wouldn't pass a risk assessment back home.

"That's not why we don't bring anyone here. The locals want to keep it private."

Moments later, Sean pulled up into a clearing. Stopping up next to him, my mouth to fall open in awe. Before us was a waterfall fed lagoon, isolated from the world by tall mountains and forest.

Dismounting, Sean tied the reins of his horse to a tree before helping me to dismount. He walked to the edge of the lagoon, pulled off his shirt, kicked his shoes off, and dived in.

Following suit, I stripped to my bikini and jumped in. The water was cool and clean. When I surfaced, I laughed. "This is amazing!" Sean smiled, his eyes focused on me. Treading water while I turned, taking it all in. "I've never seen anything this beautiful in person."

"Me neither," Sean murmured. Turning to face him, I realized his eyes were intent on me. He swam closer to me, and for a moment, I thought he was going to wrap me in his arms and kiss me. "Come on; you've got to experience it properly," he encouraged, as he swam by me.

I swam after him, towards the waterfall and then to the rocks to one side. "The current is too strong to get close to the fall," Sean explained. "It'd pummel you to death on the rocks beneath with the force of it." Climbing onto the rocks, Sean held out his hand to me. "But there is another way to get close."

Leading me across the rocks, we found around a tiny goat path. This led us in behind the curtain of water to a small eroded rock shelf hidden by the waterfall. It was darker here; the water shutting out most of the light, and the roar of the water making it hard to hear anything.

Standing back, Sean watched me take it in. Reaching out my hand to feel the water, I got the off-spray, not the direct fall. Letting it fill my cupped hands, I drank the clean water. "What does it taste like?" Sean yelled over the roar of the water. There was a smile trying to escape his lips.

Slipping my hand into his hair, I pulled his mouth to mine. Our lips met, pinched, and opened. Sean's tongue delved into my mouth, tasting, dueling with my tongue. His hands feeling over the damp skin of my back and hips as our bodies pressed against each other.

We pulled back, our breathing a bit labored from the passionate kiss. Sean closed his eyes and leaned his forehead to mine. His mouth moved in the shape of words, talking to me, but I couldn't hear him over the water. Removing himself a moment later, he left me there.

Inhaling, I closed my eyes. Sean didn't fraternize with customers, and I took him to be a very moral man. I was sure that's what he'd reiterated after the kiss, that he couldn't do that with me. What was I thinking? I was leaving at lunchtime tomorrow to board a cruise ship and sail home. I should enjoy the day, say goodbye to him tonight, and go on my way tomorrow.

Exhaling, I opened my eyes and moved out from behind the curtain of water. Sean was swimming back across the lagoon to the horses. Slipping back into the water, I swam across the lagoon. Sean helped me out on the other side, then turned and pulled his shirt on.

"Thank you for showing me this place," I broke the silence between us. Starting to dress, I kept my back to Sean as I did. "It just topped my best five experiences."

"There's another place I want to show you," Sean offered as he mounted his horse.

"Thank you, but I've had enough for today. I'd like to have a rest before dinner." When I threw myself into the saddle, Sean's eyes dimmed with disappointment. "You don't have to return to the hotel with me; I can find my way back."

Shaking his head, Sean moved his horse forward onto the trail. "I'll see you back."

We arrived at the stables an hour later, and the staff took my horse from me. "Thank you again," I smiled at Sean, holding my hand out. Sean took it, his lips twitching with amusement. "We probably won't see each other again before I leave, so, it was nice meeting you."

"Have dinner with me?"

"I should spend some time with my sisters-"

"You're going to be stuck on a boat with them for the next week and a half," Sean cut in. "Have dinner with me? Please?" A small lilt in his voice revealing the subtle plea in the request.

"Where, what time?"

"Lobby at six," Sean decided, without even having to think about it.

"I'll see you then." Making my way back to my room, I showered and changed ready for dinner, then I collapsed on my bed for a nap.

The room phone woke me a little later. Opening my eyes, I saw the time and cursed. "Hello?" I answered, pulling myself from the heavy clutches of the bed.

"Am I being stood up?" Sean asked.

"No, God, I'm sorry, I fell asleep. I'll be down in a minute."

Sean chuckled. "Bring a jacket. I'll meet you out front."

Arriving out the front of the hotel, I found Sean sitting astride a motorbike. Peering down at the dress I wore, I looked back to him questioningly. "This is Hawaii, Holly," Sean answered my unspoken question, handing me a helmet.

Pulling my jacket on, I strapped on the helmet, and threw my leg over behind him. Gripping his waist, I tried not to squeal when he revved the engine and the bike shot forward. We rode to Sunset Point and sat there watching the sunset. Not a word said between us, and I found that silence was comfortable around Sean. After the sun dropped below the horizon, Sean rode us back to the resort. He took the scenic route which was beautiful at night.

When we got back to the resort, we ate dinner in the upscale restaurant. We discussed our favorite water sports and Sean's favorite things to do on his weekends. Afterwards, we went for a walk along the beach.

"How about you, Holly?" Sean asked. We'd run out of places and things to do in Hawaii. "What do you do for leisure at home?"

"I used to swim laps on my meal break when I was on night shift, and yoga on my days off."

"You never get out and travel? I've heard Australia is an amazing country for sight-seeing?" Sean challenged.

"I saw a lot of the cities growing up. My dad traveled a lot for work and the occasional family holiday. This is my first holiday in five years. I worked weekends till recently, so I haven't had time to do much else."

We stopped walking and looked out at the moon across the water. It felt familiar. Searching for a landmark, I realized we were standing on the same spot of the beach as last night. Right outside Sean's beach cottage. The cool breeze blowing off the water reminded us that spring had only just arrived in this part of the world.

Stepping closer, Sean wrapped his arms around me to keep me warm. "Holly, I don't want you to leave tomorrow," Sean murmured to my hair. Exhaling, I closed my eyes. I felt the same. "Stay," Sean requested as he turned me to face him. "For the length of the cruise, for as long as you can. I'll pay your ticket home, but I want this time with you. Truthfully, I think you need a longer holiday."

I met Sean's eyes, so determined in what he was asking of me. "If I agree?"

"Well, there's this." Lowering his mouth, Sean kissed me. He was tender, tentative in his exploration of my lips. "There will be more sunsets," he whispered. He kissed a trail along my jaw to my ear. "We can explore more of Hawaii together. I'll take time off work to be with you," he assured. Dropping my head back, I enjoyed the wet trail his mouth created down the side of my neck. "Then at night…" Lifting his face above mine, Sean waited for me to open my eyes. When I met his gaze, my smile equaled the one in his eyes. "There will be movies and popcorn."

"Oh, you know how to woo a girl," I simpered.

"Is that a yes?"

Sobering, I withdrew from his affection. "You're suggesting a few more weeks. A holiday romance. At the end, I fly home and leave you as a happy memory?"

"I'm asking for a few more weeks, but at the end, the options will depend on both of us," Sean left it open.

"I'd love to, Sean, but this place is above my price range for that long a stay, even with you paying my ticket home."

"Holly, you'd still be checking out of the hotel tomorrow, and my bed doesn't cost you a thing," he dismissed my excuse. When I lifted a brow, Sean shook his head. "While I hope you want to do that, I don't expect it, Holly. We've shared a bed before."

"My sisters will have something to say about this. You know that, right?" I reminded him I wasn't alone on this trip.

Stepping back, taking my hand in his, Sean walked us to his cottage. "You're a grown woman, Holly. You've been making your own decisions for a long time now. They'll have to accept whatever you decide."

My sisters had never seen me as able to make my own decisions. Leading me into his cottage, the door clicked shut behind us. Removing my jacket, I kicked off my shoes as I stepped inside. Catching my shoulders in his hands, Sean pressed his body against my back, his breath tickling my ear. "Say you'll stay?"

"Two weeks," I murmured.

Sean's hot lips kissed down the side of my neck, his hands rubbing down my arms then encircling my waist. "You said you had a month's leave, Holly. That's three more weeks." His strong hands caressed over my abdomen. His lips pinched my neck as Sean's hands split. One traveling north, the other south.

"Two weeks is a respectable holiday fling, anything longer is more," I defended. A gasp escaped me as Sean's southern hand found the bare skin of my thigh.

Pulling back, Sean turned me to face him and cupped my face in his hands. "I want the more." His mouth captured mine in the kiss to end all kisses. Hard and passionate, he slid his tongue between my lips.

Butterflies swirled through my stomach. Muscles through my abdomen and pelvis contracted. Nerves fired down my legs till my toes curled and my body lurched forward to be closer to Sean.

Wrapping my arms around him, I pulled his body hard to mine. When his hands grabbed my arse, I jumped into his hold without a second thought.

Sean kissed me all the way to his bedroom. He refused to relinquish my mouth even when he lowered my legs to the ground and slid my knickers down my thighs.

My hands were tugging at his belt, shoving his clothes from his body. We broke the kiss to lift his shirt over his head, my dress and bra joining it on the floor a moment later. By the time Sean located my pearl and started tapping out his intentions, I was panting.

Sean moved us to lay on his bed. His fingers rubbed and stroked me, the hard pressure of his palm on my clit making me bite my lip. Spreading my thighs wider as the friction built a burning heat. When the tips of his fingers separated my moist folds, I arched and moaned as he made me crave more.

My fingers caressed over the hard lines of his tanned skin. Skimming the surface, I enjoyed the way Sean moaned in response. Brushing against his hardness, I felt the smooth length against the side of my hand. Turning my wrist, I grasped him, wrapping my fingers and twisting my hands over him. Sean grunted, his hips pushing forward with force. With a final kiss, Sean opened the drawer of his bedside table, ripped open a condom and rolled it on. He lowered himself between my welcoming thighs, and I helped guide him to my molten core.

Taking the invitation, Sean thrust forward. He took three goes to convince my body he needed more space than already on offer. Gripping his firm arse, I'm encouraged him while seeking something secure to hold me in this reality.

There was nothing hesitant in the way Sean delved into me, or in how I gave myself over to him. I was deeply attracted to him. And I was sick of denying myself what I wanted.

Sean lifted one of my legs up, bending it over his bicep so he could drive deeper. Throwing my head back, I gripped the bed-head to prevent scratching him up, my fingers gripping the wrought iron with all my strength. Capturing my mouth, Sean kissed me till I was breathless. Dropping his mouth to my breast, he changed the angle of his body. I bit my lip to prevent vocalizing how good it felt. Years of internalizing my pleasure and controlling my reactions natural to me now.

Sean lifted his head. Slowing his body, he turned his thrusts into circles, punctuated by a sharp push on the in, to reach as deep as he could. Clenching my jaw, I closed my eyes. Grunting, Sean put his hand to my mouth. "Open," he ordered.

Complying, I sucked his thumb into my mouth. Swearing, Sean thrust a little faster. Swelling inside me, his body demanded I open further to his need. I turned my head to hinder the moan that was building. As I pressed my lips together around his thumb, Sean used his hand to force my mouth open and drove his hips forward. I moaned audibly, a tension I hadn't even recognized I was holding escaping into the room. God, it felt good to let it out.

"That's more like it, Holly. You don't have to be quiet here. I want to hear you."

When I moaned again, Sean grinned and kissed me. Moving his mouth to my breast, I was climaxing for him seconds later. Opening my lips, I let Sean know how hard I was cumming. Years of pent up restriction and fear flying free and leaving me limp, and the most relaxed I'd been in two years. Clenching his eyes and gritting his jaw, Sean's entire body seized. Grunting with each thrust, Sean forced his body to finish what it started. Drawing the pleasure out longer for both of us.

When he collapsed beside me, we took a minute to catch our breaths while staring at the ceiling. "Three weeks," Sean choked, clearing his throat. "I want the three weeks."

Rolling to my side I kissed his chest. The smile on my face hurting my cheeks, using muscles it felt like I hadn't activated since I was a child. I couldn't remember being this happy for a long time. Tucking me under his arm, Sean waited for my reply. Having just had the best orgasm of my life, was I going to say no?

"I best go book my flight."

CHAPTER SEVEN

Grumbling, I hid my head under the pillow to drown out the sound of the phone ringing. "Hello?" Sean's voice answered sleepily. "That's okay, Henry, my alarm will go off shortly. Is there a problem?" Sean ran a hand down my naked back, over my rear, and between my thighs to caress me. "No, she's not missing. Miss Claire was inquiring about the best places to watch the sunrise from yesterday. She intended to set out early to take advantage of her last morning as a guest of the Cassidy Resort."

I bit my lip on a moan as Sean's fingers sunk into me to massage my good spot. "Assure her sister that if Miss Claire hasn't surfaced by the end of breakfast, we'll go looking for her. Thanks, Henry." Sean hung up.

"Lier," I accused from beneath my pillow.

"Not at all. From where you are lying, you have an amazing view of the sunrise." The bedside table drawer opened and closed. The distinct sound of a foil wrapping tearing filled the silence.

Lifting the pillow, I peeked out at the window. I blinked once, twice, then lifted my head to watch the sky changing color. It was beautiful. The gray light of dawn growing lighter over the ocean outside.

Sean shifted between my thighs behind me. "Beautiful isn't it?" He kissed across my shoulders. "Just like you." He kissed my cheek and nibbled my ear.

Pressing himself into me, Sean moved like the tide,

surging deeper and deeper with each wave. Gold light lit up the horizon, marbling the gray sky with blues and pinks. Gripping the bed, I closed my eyes a moment, lifting my hips to feel more of Sean.

"Watch it, it's beautiful," Sean breathed in my ear.

"You're not watching it."

"I've seen it for ten years. The beauty of you cumming in the morning, that's something new, but equally as captivating."

Withdrawing, Sean surged forward again, still not reaching full tide. The sky was sapphire on gold. The gold was melting, bleeding into the sapphire, blending to aquamarine. As the morning broke free of the night's clutches, Sean filled me. His strokes deep and not so purposeful as he lost himself to the brilliance of my dawning.

"Let me hear it, Holly," Sean demanded when I fell into the habit of keeping quiet.

Opening my mouth, I sang along with the birds outside, praising the sunrise. Swept up by the wave of pleasure, Sean surged through the ocean of climax to crash upon my back breathless. He kissed me deeply before he removed himself to dispose of the condom, then returned to lie beside me.

"That was the best sunrise I've seen in ten years," Sean declared. "I want to start every morning like that."

Chuckling, I turned my head to watch him. Sean turned his face to me, and his lips turned up into a smile.

"You know what I've liked most about last night and this morning?" I challenged. Sean's smile faded a little at my tone, and he rolled his body towards me. "We were both naked, and we did it in bed." Smiling, I closed my eyes, snuggling into the comfort. "It's been eight years since I've had sex naked, in a bed."

When I opened my eyes, Sean considered me with raised brows. "How have you been doing it with your casual liaison?"

"Fully dressed, and quickly, against the wall, or the desk," I admitted.

"You were having sex at work?"

"Yes, but never during my shift."

"So, the sexual harassment...?"

"My new manager found out and tried to blackmail me into extending him the same courtesy." Watching Sean, I wondered if my admission changed his impression of me. "Do you still want me to stay?"

Sean caressed my face. "You think I'm going to throw you out of my bed because your former boss was too stupid to treat you right?"

I jolted back from his reach. "How did you know it was my boss?"

Sean looked guilty. "I overheard your sisters discussing it. Something about what a scandal it would be if it came out. They felt the media would be all over it if they found out, and they were deciding if they should let your parents know."

I jumped up from the bed. "They what?"

"I guess your boss is someone important in your country. Your sisters worried about the backlash." Sitting up, Sean observed my reaction.

"He's the son of someone, and a perpetual bachelor," I groaned. "That I was in a two-year long affair with him would be front-page news. It's the longest relationship he's ever had." Pacing, annoyed with my sisters, and worried Sean would judge me for getting involved with my boss.

"It probably lasted as long as it did because it was secret," Sean suggested. "You were also a subordinate who he could take advantage of, and manipulate. If you asked for something more serious, you could be made redundant. He could get rid of you without the grit of a relationship ending."

"You make it sound like he was using me."

Sean raised a brow. "You said it yourself; you thought you meant more than it appears he did. You had to quit your job, Holly."

I stopped pacing and swiped at the moisture leaking onto my cheek. Closing my eyes, I steadied myself. "He wouldn't have let it end, if I'd stayed. He didn't want the affair to end, but he didn't want a relationship with me either. If I didn't leave, he would have seduced me again, and I wanted to date and have a relationship. I've craved what you've given me in the last twenty-four hours for a decade. I didn't even realize how badly I wanted it till I met you."

Throwing the sheet back, Sean stood, taking me in his arms. "Strangely enough, I didn't realize how much I missed it until you walked into my hotel and smiled at me."

Meeting Sean's eyes, I stepped back fearfully. "You can't look at me like that, Sean. Three weeks. That's all I agreed too."

Sean reeled me back into his grasp, his hands caressing my hair, forcing me to meet his eyes. "You agreed to three weeks and to see where it goes from there," Sean reminded me. "A lot can happen in three weeks, Holly."

"My world fell apart in a day, Sean. I'm uncertain I'm up for any more change right now."

Sean rested his forehead against mine. His alarm started shrieking across the room. With a huff, Sean released me and silenced the alarm. "I'm going for a surf before work. Did you want to join me?"

"My swimmers are at the hotel. I should go and pack, and spend the morning with my sisters." Sean look away rejected. "Tomorrow morning, definitely."

Sean's lips twitched in a smile. Tugging me toward him, he kissed me deeply. "Check out, then bring your stuff down here." Opening the drawer next to his bed, Sean handed me a key on a key ring.

I held it up. "You keep a spare for your flings?"

"I had it cut yesterday while you slept," Sean countered. "I decided after the waterfall, that I couldn't let you leave today. I planned, hopeful that you'd give this a chance."

"My sister considers you a rebound." In my head, I worried how intensely I already felt about Sean.

"Officially, you would be my rebound also," Sean offered.

Meeting his eyes, fear clenched my stomach in its irrepressible fist. "This might hurt."

Nodding, Sean took my face in his hands. "I'm betting it will." He kissed me slowly, emotionally. Sean didn't bother with surfing. Our bodies fell back to the bed, where we expressed our emotions to each other physically.

As we walked back to the resort together, Sean took my hand. It felt nice to walk connected like that. I tried to drop his hand before entering the lobby, not wanting his staff to see. Sean held it tighter.

"They are going to know in a matter of days you're staying with me, Holly. There's no point playing denial games."

He was right. When we walked inside and his staff noticed with wide eyes and wider mouths, I felt way too self-conscious. Sean cleared his throat as we passed to the elevator, and everyone snapped out of it, returning to their work.

"You're going to be the gossip today," I warned.

"I'm a single man who doesn't indulge in illicit affairs with women who hit on me," Sean declared. "I'm gossiped about already."

"It's about to be so much worse," I warned humored.

Sean grinned releasing me into the elevator. "Go pack your stuff and say goodbye to your sisters, Holly. I'm going to make the rumor mill burn with my plans for you."

I blushed as the elevator doors closed, separating me from Sean. Nervous and excited all at once, I had what my mother used to call the jitters. My nerves were on edge, the thought of eating made my stomach turn, and I couldn't stop smiling. The next three weeks could be a great adventure I'd remember for the rest of my life fondly. Or, it would be my biggest heartbreak.

Was I stupid for hoping for an amazing three weeks that I could walk away from with a smile and fond memories? Probably. Still, it was the about time I took what I'd waited two years for with Benjamin.

*****

"You what?" Sadie screeched across the breakfast table.

"Calm down," I shushed her.

"Calm down? Overnight you've decided overnight to

cancel your cruise home and go island jumping. By yourself."

"I'm a grown adult, Sadie. I can go on holiday by myself," I dismissed her concerns.

Sadie made a noise that made it obvious she disagreed. "Sadie," Nichola shook her head. Her eyes turned to me, so like our mother. "Are you sure about this, Holly? You can't get your money back on the cruise this late."

"Well, I was crashing in your room and didn't pay for the accommodation only boarding. So, the company was happy to reimburse me. That will pay for my flight home instead."

Sean purchased my ticket home before I contacted my friend who I'd booked the cruise through. I was over the moon she got me a refund, as that was my spending money for the next three weeks.

"This is stupid, just get on the boat," Sadie decided.

"You're not hearing me. I've already booked a flight home and canceled my cruise. They wouldn't let me on the boat home if I tried," I clarified the situation for them. "I've enjoyed spending time with you both, but it might be years before I take another holiday like this again. I want to see the rest of Hawaii, enjoy more of the recreation, and I don't know, live, for the rest of my holiday."

"You're reckless, stupid, and immature," Sadie lectured.

"Yeah, well, I guess mum and dad were right about me," I snapped. "I can't believe you have the gall to call me reckless."

"I'm your older sister," Sadie scolded.

"And such a great role model. There's a guy over there who looks like he needs a blow-job. Why don't you let him and his friends fuck your every orifice and film it? Nothing reckless about that." I stormed off leaving Sadie and Nichola staring after me mouths wide open.

Muttering to myself angrily all the way back to my room, I was there two minutes before someone knocked at the door. "Who is it?"

"Sean Cassidy, the manager," he sounded like he was laughing. I opened the door sheepishly. "I noticed you stormed out of the restaurant. Was there a problem with breakfast?" Sean asked professionally, a smile tugging at the side of his lips.

Grabbing him by the collar, I pulled him into my room. The door slam shut as I pushed Sean against the wall and started kissing him heatedly. Sean's hands were all over me. He undressed me while I pulled his clothes free from his outdoors-man physique.

"Jesus, Holly," Sean breathed. "I'm working. I just came to make sure you're okay?"

"I'm not okay," I murmured. "I need you inside me."

Sean didn't waste another word arguing. "Condom?" Sean requested as we maneuvered through the lounge to the bed.

"Fuck," I muttered, breaking away for a second in annoyance.

"Holly?"

"I'm not used to needing them."

"Because rushed office sex doesn't allow for practicing safe sex," Sean nodded understanding.

"I'm clean, and I'm on birth control."

Sean took my face in his hands. "I'm clean, and I'm sensible." Sean kissed me, deep, but quick, then collected his clothes and dressed.

"Wait, so that means we're not doing this?" I asked surprised.

"Not right now, no. You're upset and angry. You are not in the state to make wise decisions about unsafe practices."

"Excuse me?"

Sean sighed, righting his uniform. Collecting my clothes, he walked towards me. "You have nothing but my word that I'm clean, Holly. What happens if, for some reason or another, your contraception didn't work?" Sean caressed my cheek. "Major life choices made for five minutes of angry sex."

Taking my clothes, I turned my back to redress. "Why does everyone have the ability to make me feel like a stupid child?"

"I'm older than you, Holly. The same with your siblings. I

guess your former boss was older still," Sean spoke carefully. "I've seen people's lives turned upside down by one thoughtless moment. While I'm all for spontaneity, I'd prefer you not to leave here with a life-altering regret."

Turning me around to face him, Sean wiped the wetness from my cheeks with his thumb and kissed me. "Go settle in at my place, enjoy your afternoon, and come up to the resort and have dinner with me. Tonight, I promise I'll fuck you so hard you'll struggle to walk tomorrow."

"You better," I grumbled.

Sean smirked. "We wouldn't want to prove your sister right about you being reckless."

I gapped at him. "How did you know that?"

Sean chuckled. "My staff called me to deal with a loud dispute in the restaurant. I was on my way to your table to calm the fight down when you suggested your sister start a gang-bang and stormed out."

Embarrassed, I sat on the bed. I'd become one of those guests. "I didn't realize we were that loud. I apologize."

Combing his fingers through my hair, Sean used my hair to tilt my head up for his lips. "You can make it up to me tonight."

My eyes dropped to the still obvious erection in his pants. Grabbing his pants, I yanked him closer as I freed his hard-on to my lips. "I'd rather do it now."

CHAPTER EIGHT

"Are you sure?" Nichola asked as we stood in the lobby waiting for Sadie so they could catch the shuttle to the port.

"I'm sure. I want to stay for a few more weeks and experience as much as I can."

Nichola's eyes went over my shoulder. Turning to see that Sean was at the front desk talking to his staff, I blushed. "Well, I can't say that it's not worth experiencing," Nichola sighed.

When I met Nichola's eyes, we laughed. "I swear, I am going to be Island hopping and seeing as much as I can." Nichola raised a brow. "I didn't say I'd be doing it alone."

Nichola pulled me into a hug. "Be safe, Holly. Call me when you get home, and we'll organize Bridesmaids dresses."

"Again?" I whined.

"You're my sister, Holly, you have to be my bridesmaid," Nichola insisted.

She released me from the hug as Sadie stomped into the lobby and glared at me. "Try not to be stupid," she scowled, then walked out to get on the shuttle bus.

Nichola gave me a side hug. "You're not stupid, Holly. Never have been. Enjoy the holiday."

Nichola went to join Sadie, scolding her when she took the seat next to her. Sadie held up her hand to gesture she wasn't listening and turned her attention to the window. Yeah, Sadie had serious middle child syndrome.

Cassidy

Waving as the bus pulled away, I collected my bag and headed down the path for the beach cottages. Letting myself into Sean's place, hung my dress from the symphony in his wardrobe so it wouldn't crease. I'd packed it in for the formal dinner on the cruise. Heading to the beach, I wanted the ocean to wash away my cares. Renting a board, I surfed the morning away.

After a shower at Sean's, I went to Sean's favorite beach shack for lunch. Back at the hotel, I went to the lobby to organize what else I would see or do this week. "Afternoon, Miss Claire, I didn't realize you were still here?"

Looking up, I smiled at the concierge. "Afternoon, Henry. Yes, I decided to stay for a few more weeks to fully experience this wonderful place."

Henry looked surprised. "But you checked out of your room?"

He had a very valid point. "I did." I wasn't exactly comfortable pointing out I was staying with his boss. "I'm staying in one of the cottages with a friend." Henry's brow frowned, no doubt aware of everyone staying in the cottages. "Not permanently. Just a couple of days here to explore this island, and then I'll be island hopping."

"Oh!" Henry looked unsure. His eyes told me he was trying to work out with which guest I was staying. "Well, is there something I can assist you with?"

Holding up one of the brochures, I grinned. "A booking on the north shore zip line for tomorrow please?"

Henry took the brochure. "Morning or afternoon?"

"Whenever there is availability."

"I'll give them a call for you, Miss Claire. If you tell me which cottage you are in, I'll call you with the time."

It was a good try. "I'm going to Waikiki to do the bicycle tour, so let me know when I come up for dinner."

Henry almost huffed in annoyance. Winking at him, I turned to leave when he blushed. Sean was standing smiling at us. "Everything alright, Henry?"

"Of course, Sean, just helping Miss Claire make a booking."

"I'll take over. I need you to visit Mr. Harrington and see to his most recent request please." Sean handed Henry a folded piece of paper.

"Yes, Sean." Henry swapped Sean the brochure for the piece of paper. "Miss Claire would like to do the zip line at some stage tomorrow."

Nodding, Sean waited for Henry to walk away. "So, the zip line?"

"I didn't know how quickly you'd be able to organize leave. So, I thought I would spend the next few days doing all the local stuff." My eyes drinking in the gorgeous man who was keeping a respectable distance from me.

"I've informed my staff I'll be on leave from Wednesday." Reaching over the desk, Sean took the other brochures from me, letting his hand linger on mine a minute as he did. "Is this everything you want to do?"

"So far. I'm sure you'll have plenty more ideas of how best to spend my three weeks here?"

Sean gave me a lopsided grin. "I have an idea about tonight, that's for sure."

"Movie marathon?"

Sean leaned toward me. "I thought that was your sister's thing? But, if you want me to film it, I won't object to having a way to reflect on our time together."

"Never going to happen."

Sean pouted. "Okay, well, then no movies," he winked. "I'll book you into these, and I'll book us into a few more." He waved the brochures standing straight and moving to the phone.

"Henry wants to know where I'm staying now." Sean lifted a brow. "I told him I'm staying with a friend in the cottages."

"As sweet as it is that you're trying to protect my reputation, I'm pretty sure our arrival this morning let that cat out of the bag."

"Really?" I smirked stepping closer.

Meeting my eyes, Sean looked a bit frightened. "You look very dangerous right now, Holly."

"I want to kiss you."

Sean's eyes lit up. "As much as I want that too, while I'm working, I prefer to conduct myself professionally." Sean smiled watching me. "But you knew that?"

Nodding, I took a step back. "I do," I assured, taking another step back, still smiling at Sean. Over his shoulder, I spotted Henry approaching. "Well, I'm off to go bike riding, I'll see you at dinner?"

"I'll meet you here at six."

"Thank you, Mr. Cassidy," I farewelled sweetly.

Sean got this humored look on his face with my formal farewell. Then Henry was beside him and understanding dawned. Winking, I went out to catch a ride into Honolulu.

*****

The guided bicycle tour was an eight-mile cruise through Waikiki culture and history. The route took us through green parks, past white-sand beaches, and into the heart of Honolulu.

We started by heading along a car-free path toward Kahi Hali'a Aloha. A burial mound holding skeletons dug up during various Waikiki construction projects. We rode along a waterfront path to the Waikiki Aquarium. The second-oldest aquarium in the United States. We rode by the Waikiki Natatorium War Memorial swimming pool. It was built on Kaimana Beach to honor the men and women who served in World War I.

After cruising along the beach, the tour headed to Kapiolani Park. The largest and oldest public park in Hawaii, it is a popular meeting point for parades and festivals. Next, we rolled by the Honolulu Zoo and stopped for a delicious soft-serve ice cream.

We rounded off the tour by heading past Fort DeRussy, the Hawaii Army Museum, Cassidy's Point, and Ala Wai Harbor. Finally, we rode the car-free path, past the Ala Wai golf course and along Kapahulu Avenue to where the tour began.

It was a well thought out tour, and beat the usual stand and shuffle tours that my sisters seemed to enjoy. I jumped on the shuttle bus back to the resort and went for a shower and rest before dinner. After a full day of exercise, my legs were telling me about it, but I was happy.

Arriving in the lobby right on six, I took a seat. Sean wasn't in the lobby, and, knowing what managing a hotel consisted of, I decided to wait until he was free to eat. "Miss Claire," Henry greeted. "Can I help you with something?"

"No, thank you, Henry. I'm waiting for my dinner date."

"Did Sean give you the information about the zip line tomorrow?"

"Not yet. Mr. Cassidy told me he'd give that to me when I came up for dinner tonight," I assured, before looking out the window. "I might sit by the pool to watch the sunset. Could you let Mr. Cassidy know where to find me?"

"Of course. And, your dinner date?"

I resisted a chuckle. Henry's eyes told me he knew with whom I was having dinner. "Him too." I walked off before he could press for me to confirm his suspicions.

Finding a seat overlooking the beach, I watched the colors start to change ready for sunset. "Can I get you something?" The poolside waitress asked.

"Hydration in a glass would be wonderful please."

"Of course, what room should I charge it to?"

Crap. "I'll pay cash." Pulling out a few bills, I handed it to the waitress. Laying back, I watched the sun's descent, my eyelids racing it.

"There you are." The waitress placed the drink on the table next to me, my change with it.

"Thank you." Sitting a bit straighter, I tipped the waitress, and started drinking. My drink was gone by the time the sun disappeared from the sky, and my stomach was complaining. Realizing it was an hour and a half past the time Sean said to meet him, I decided I was going solo for dinner tonight. Whatever the issue he was dealing with must be serious.

Making my way to the outdoor bar, I found a table and browsed the menu. The bar served more casual meals than the restaurant, and with how hungry I was, that would do if it meant it was fast.

"Can I get you another drink, Miss Claire?"

Cassidy

I smiled up at the waitress. Her name tag read Bee. "Is that your real name?"

She smiled, observing her name tag. "Short for Beatrice. I hate people calling me by my full name."

"I hate people using my surname. Anything connecting me to my family's fame is unwelcome. Call me Holly?"

Bee smiled. "Can I get you something, Holly?"

"I'd love the Bird and Brie burger with battered beer fries and a Coke please."

"Aioli?"

"Definitely." I smiled handing her my card. "Credit please."

Bee took my card and order and walked away. She returned with my Coke and card a few minutes later. Sean took the seat opposite me as she did. "I'm sorry, Holly," Sean sounded as exhausted as I felt. "Drink up, and we'll go get dinner."

"I've ordered. I was starving."

Instead of annoyance, Sean lifted his eyes to Bee, who seemed frozen on the spot. "Double bacon and beef meal please, Bee. Charge our meals to me please."

"Holly has already paid for her meal, Mr. Cassidy." Bee squirmed. There is no better word for it. The pretty waitress smitten for her boss.

"Has she?" Sean raised a brow at me.

"I agreed to stay, I didn't say you could support me while I'm here."

Bee's eyes widened. "Coke for your drink, Mr. Cassidy?"

"Beer please, Bee. I'm in serious need of beer," Sean answered, unbuttoning his collar and removing his blazer.

"Yes, Mr. Cassidy."

I waited till we were alone. "That girl has a serious crush on you. If she doesn't spit in my food, I'll be surprised."

Sean ignored my comment. "I'm sorry; we had an incident."

"I gathered," I shrugged off his concern. "I've worked the industry long enough to know how it goes, Sean, don't fret. Are you finished for the night?"

"Hell, yes," Sean stifled a yawn. He looked at me; then his eyes went to the bar. "Back in a second," he excused as he stood and went to the bar. He came back with his beer and took his seat. "I've asked for our meals to be takeaway. I want to go home and change. Then we are going to sit and watch some crappy movie that requires no brain function from me."

"Go have a shower. I'll bring dinner down when it's ready."

Sean threw back his beer, sculling it. When it was empty, he sighed and met my eyes. "Can't leave the bar with any drinks," he explained before standing. "Thank you for being understanding." Leaning across the table, Sean threaded his hand into my hair and kissed me passionately. It was a short, but intent kiss that left me wanting more. Sean pulled back. "I'll see you in a few minutes."

Sean grab up his blazer and walked to the bar. He gave the staff instruction before he made his way toward the beach. The staff all smiled at me, eyes insinuating enough to make me blush. Well, that was that.

CHAPTER NINE

The zip line was exhilarating. The Eco-adventure started with a four-wheel-drive down a rugged dirt road. While we walked along an elevated platform in the trees, the guide shared tips for getting the most out of the experience.

All seven lines of the course we're dual lines, so many on tour raced their friends to the end. Since I was by myself, I enjoyed the spectacular surroundings as I glided over the forest floor below. The views looked out at fields of tropical fruit and to the white sands and azure waters of the coast.

There were various rope challenges as well. I had a ball climbing, rappelling, and crossing rope bridges between platforms. On top of this morning's wake up with Sean, followed by a surf, my body was sore by the end of the afternoon tour.

When I arrived at the lobby for dinner, I found the first available seat and damn well planted my tired arse in it. "You look wiped," Sean chuckled as he dropped into the seat beside me.

"Yep, you'll be doing all the work in bed tonight." I leaned against him. "I'm going to lie back and think of England."

Sean laughed. "England?"

"I come from a British colony, Sean. Sex was a husband's right, but women weren't to enjoy it. Oh, no, we women were to lay back and think of England or pray to the Virgin Mary."

"Well, that explains the praying you do," Sean teased. I tickled his side and he jolted away. "No, seriously, Holly, you make sex a devoted spiritual experience." He moved his mouth to my ear. "Especially when you stop biting your lip and let me hear you."

Blushing like a Hawaiian sunset, I tried to hide in my shoulders. "I like what you do to me."

Sean smiled and moved his face a little closer. "I enjoy the way you react to me. You are sort of zero to a hundred in one caress."

"Years of quickies train your body that if you're going to get off, it needs to get there fast," I confessed. "Though, the way you work me seems to make getting there way more intense."

Sean adjusted the way he was sitting. "If I weren't still on shift for another three hours, I'd be suggesting we skip dinner and get room service later."

Biting my lip, I closed my eyes as I imagined racing back to Sean's place and stripping him. My thighs ached as I squeezed them and my hands hurt where I gripped my skirt. Damn clinging to ropes half the day. "Holly?"

I opened one eye to peek at Sean. "I'm a little sore, so as lovely as that sounds, dinner and a rest sound better."

Sean took my hand in his. "Then let's eat before someone decides to O.D. again."

I let Sean lead me to the dining room. "Is that what happened last night?"

Sean looked at me. "Yeah, though I shouldn't have told you that."

"Please, who am I going to tell?"

Sean smiled. "Good point." He kissed the top of my head as we walked. "We have an American celebrity staying with us. Yesterday, they partied a little hard. Their manager called for help, but wouldn't let us call an ambulance," Sean revealed. "This celebrity has a reputation that drugs and whoring would jeopardize. So, I had to call a friend for a favor. She's a private doctor here and is very good at keeping her mouth shut. She saved the client, and once they were stable, presented the manager with the bill. They weren't impressed with her charges and tried to insist we cover the fee."

"Ouch!" I cringed. "Please tell me you didn't?"

"God, no. That's a staff member's annual wage. I'd have to let someone go, and I'm very happy with my staff, so no," Sean answered. "I'd warned the manager that she was expensive. They said they didn't care. I told the manager they could sort it out with the doctor. Bells, my friend, told the manager they could accept the bill, or she could call the police."

"Which means public knowledge, so they won't do that," I acknowledged.

"That's right," Sean agreed. In the restaurant, we were led to our table and shown the specials.

"So, everything got sorted in the end?"

"In the end, yes," Sean nodded.

We placed our orders. I went for high protein to counteract the day's activities. "When I get back, I'm going to spend every weekend out and doing something, even if it's bike riding around Centennial Park."

Sean smirked. "Feel a little unfit, do we? Cause you don't look it." Sean's eyes indulged in the view down my sundress.

"No, it's the after ache that's killing me." Clasping my hands behind my chair, I stretched. "But the endorphins from exercising, they should take my mind off the lack of sex."

"Lack of sex?" Sean cocked a brow, looking trapped between offended and humored.

"Yeah, because I can't deny I'm going to miss you when I get home. My body especially will, but I'm not going to be rushing into anything, so I'll need to burn the energy off somehow." I considered my cutlery. "Maybe I can convince Roger to let me use the hotel pool either before or after my shift every day for laps." Lifting my eyes to Sean, I appraised his broad shoulders. "Maybe twice a day."

"Roger?" Sean asked with a chuckle.

"My new boss. Sweet guy. You know what I like about him most?" Sean frowned shaking his head. "His wife. She's wonderful and pregnant with child number three. It's so obvious they adore each other, so I'll never have to worry about him trying to bend me over my desk." I said the last with a little too much venom, and a little louder than needed for Sean to hear.

Sean's eyebrows were in his hair. He cleared his throat and the waiter, whose brows were equally as high, placed our entrees on the table. "Sorry, I got a bit carried away."

Sean waited for us to be alone again. "So, you're working for another hotel?"

I blinked, surprised that's what Sean wanted to discuss. "Yes, where else would I work?"

"Well, I thought you might be working as a reviewer," Sean mentioned carefully. "I saw some of the stuff you'd written about your initial impression of my resort here. The things you felt needed fixing, what worked and what didn't."

I continued to blink at Sean. "You got all that off one glance when I dropped my book at your feet?"

"I can see a lot with a quick glimpse," Sean admitted. "You've also been writing about your experiences each day at my place. You don't write like a travel diary, you write like a reviewer. The good, the bad, the downright horrible."

"I'm not a reviewer. At least, I don't earn my keep by reviewing. The first entry in that book was when I was nine. My family traveled a lot. I loved seeing new places, seeing how different places did things. For Christmas one year, I got that notebook. It was intended to be a diary, but I started writing about my travel experiences. I've been doing it ever since."

Sean considered me. "Could I read it?"

"No. I consider it just as private as if it was a personal diary."

"I'd love to know what you think I need to fix here, Holly," Sean pushed.

"That's not a good idea," I muttered, and started eating.

Sean watched me, dropped his head and started on his meal. "Can you tell me about your new job? Are you managing a hotel?"

"No. I'm a staff manager. I'm playing intermediary

between the owner and the hotel staff. He doesn't have hospitality experience, despite his family's big name in it. He went his own way and started a business which services the hospitality industry. He started this hotel as a bet with his father."

"So, you will be the general manager?" Sean assessed.

"That and a sort of personal assistant." I didn't even consider I'd jumped two roles forward. No wonder Colin had been pissed when I'd explained my new role. The others probably picked it up right away. Even now, Sean stopped eating, looking a little perturbed.

"Did I say something wrong?"

Sean shook his head. "I saw you light up in a way I haven't yet. You love your job."

"Don't you?"

"Yes, I do, I just didn't realize you were so passionate about yours," Sean defended.

"I love being self-sufficient," I informed him. "I've spent years working my way to the position I've wanted since I was nine years old, Sean. I'm finally there. Of course, I'm going to be happy about it."

Sean nodded as our mains arrived. "So, you should," he acquiesced.

It was my turn to wait till we were alone. "You seem a little annoyed?"

Meeting my eyes, Sean shook his head and picked up his knife and fork. "I'm just not ready to think about you going home."

Reaching across the table I touched his wrist. "In case you've missed it, I'm a verifiable mess when it comes to relationships, Sean. I inevitably fuck them up. Give it three weeks, and you'll be happy to see the back of me."

Sean smirked wickedly. "Holly, I already do enjoy seeing the back of you. Or did you miss that in my kitchen this morning?"

Hot heat burnt my cheeks and I suddenly felt shy. Sean laughed, but I was already planning how to greet him when he came home this evening. First, I was stashing condoms around the cottage, so he didn't have to stop to find one.

CHAPTER TEN

"Condom," Sean panted. He went to pull away from where he knelt over me on the couch.

"Wait." I grabbed his balls to hold him in my mouth.

"I'm going to cum, Holly," Sean grunted. Searching under the cushion for the condom, I ripped it open. Sean's grip in my hair tightened as he pulled out, my saliva dripping from his tip. "Where did that come from?"

Smirking, I enjoyed his groan as I rolled it over him. "I was prepared."

Standing me up, Sean stripped me down, not that my knickers weren't already flung across the room. Sean spun me around and had me kneel on the lounge. He pushed me forward, then gave my sweet spot another licking for good measure.

"I love how you taste, Holly," Sean rumbled. He stepped in behind me. "I love your arse," he growled, dropping a quick smack to the mentioned anatomy. "Your back." He dropped kisses up my spine, teasing my entrance with his engorged head. He reached around and groped my breasts. "I had so much trouble keeping my eyes above deck that first day we met. These were bursting out of your dress and bikini top." He gripped my hair to turn my head. "And I love this pouty little mouth," he muttered, before crushing my lips in a kiss that made my knees go weak.

Releasing me, Sean jerked my hips back and thrust forward, ramming all the way home on the first stroke. I cried out, fingernails digging into the back of his couch.

Moaning with every high-friction stroke of his body in mine, I was coming five thrusts later. Sean hot on my tail. Literally.

I was still gasping for breath, eyes wide as Sean grew large and throbbed inside me. On his next thrust, I heard a popping sound, his stroke after that felt like heaven. Sean swore and pulled out as he came all over my bum and spine. "What the?"

"It was a bit too much, and the condom broke," Sean panted. He looked pained.

His cock was swollen and dripping, the remainder of the condom acting like a tourniquet. Sean rolled it off, gasping somewhere between pleasure and pain as he did. His release started dribbling down my back. Pushing him away, I raced to the bathroom, turning on the shower.

"Holly?" Sean came through the door. "Are you okay?" Sean frowned at me. "That water is cold, Holly. It's just sperm. It's nothing to freak about."

"I'm not freaking about it, I just didn't want to make a mess on your lounge," I sighed. The hot water kicked in, and I could relax.

Sean stepped into the shower with me, caressing my arms. "Are you sure that's all it is because you ran out of there pretty fast?"

My cheeks heated, Sean tipped my chin up to force me to meet his eyes. "It's silly," I murmured.

"Try me," Sean soothed.

Swallowing, my chest and neck were growing as hot as my cheeks and getting worse by the minute. "You got my arse."

Sean looked at me like I was telling an unusual joke. "You freaked out because I came on your arse?"

"No, it ran back down the crack and into my arse." I covered my face embarrassed. "It felt different."

"I take it that's a first for you?" I nodded. "You've never let a guy fuck you there?" I shook my head. "And never had a guy blow on you and felt the trickle effect?" Again, I shook my head, face still hidden in my hands. "Well, that's surprising," Sean snickered.

"Excuse me?" I dropped my hands and glared.

"Well, you've been pretty happy with everything I've done so far, even when I've got a little rough. I assumed we weren't covering new ground." Swallowing, I looked away. Sean stopped. "Wait, Holly, you've been spanked and had your hair pulled and shit before, haven't you?"

Biting my lip, I shook my head. "Actually, no. I mean I've had the thrusting hard and fast, but not the other stuff."

Sean looked me over. "But you were so into it when I grabbed your hair at the restaurant?"

"I've read books about it, and always wanted to have a guy dominate me like that, but you're the first guy who's done it."

Sean looked gobsmacked. "Did you like it?"

Stepping closer, I wrapped my arms around his neck and pulled him closer. "A little too much."

"But you didn't like my spunk going in your backend?"

"I didn't say that. I just wasn't expecting it, and it felt different," I clarified. "It was more the shock of the condom breaking that freaked me, that's all." I reached between us and stroked his flaccid member tenderly. "Did it hurt? It looked like it hurt."

"Hurt?" Sean murmured, starting to grow in my hand. "No, not physically. It was the effort of acknowledging it broke and pulling out. Especially, when what I wanted to do was cum deep inside you."

Closing my eyes, I hung my head back. "God, that makes me so horny," I admitted, pressing my thighs together.

"Me too," Sean whispered against my neck. "Can I tie you up?"

"Yes."

"Can I fuck you and then cum all over your breasts?"

"God, yes," I breathed, gasping as his finger found my clit and threw me into overdrive.

"Not tonight," Sean susurrated against my lips.

I whimpered. "Tonight, is a perfect time. I'm too tired to ride you, so tying me up is a great idea."

Sean chuckled and kissed me. "What was the movie you

were watching?"

"No idea," I breathed as his free hand tugged my nipple. In truth, I didn't pay it much attention. When Sean got home, I jumped him as he came in the door. He'd managed to laugh something about me being exhausted, before he'd yanked my underwear off, laid me back on the lounge, and gone to town on my-

"You're right," Sean muttered, breaking through my recall as he reached full hardness in my hand again. "Tonight's a good night to have you tied to my bed."

*****

I stretched like a contented cat when Sean's alarm went off. It wasn't till I tried to roll over that I realized my legs were wide apart. "What the...?"

Sean chuckled as he slipped between my thighs. I didn't get to question anything further. My breath rushed out in a moan as Sean shoved into me. Afterwards, I watched him dress for his morning surf. "You coming?" Sean asked, smiling at me.

"Twice already today, I can take a break," I sighed.

"I meant for a surf?"

"I can barely move," I moaned. "My arms feel like lead, my thighs were already sore before you kept them in the air last night, and now I'm pleasurably sore in my lady bits. I'm staying in bed." Sean came towards me. "Na ah," I shook my head. "If you want it tonight, my bat cave needs rest time."

Sean stopped. "Bat cave?"

"Dark and damp, when penetrated it makes winged things cyclone through my stomach, and for weird, unearthly sounds to come out my mouth," I educated.

Sean blinked, then knelt over me laughing. "Okay," he kissed me. "You have nothing on this morning anyway. Get some more sleep. I'll see you for breakfast." Sean kissed me again, and then he was gone, out into the early dawn and the waiting waves. I put my head down and missed breakfast entirely.

Sean left a print out with the itinerary for the next two weeks of island-hopping adventures. Today was his last day

of work until he'd be joining me, but once he did, he'd booked us in for something nearly every day. Everything I'd asked to see plus much more. Week three, however, just stated, 'you and me'.

Biting my lip on a blush, I turned my focus back to today. Swimming with dolphins followed by a hike up the Diamond Head Crater. Both took an hour, but with travel time, wouldn't get me back until just before dinner time again. I had a distinct impression that I might not be able to stand tonight.

In swimmers, shorts, a t-shirt, and enough sun cream to protect a rhino from getting burnt, I headed to the sea life park. My dolphin experience consisted of a fin shake, cheek kiss, drag across the pool, and then the dolphins made me fly. Not literally. It was a move called the foot push, but my god, it was amazing.

Still in a buzz and my wet hair pulled back in a ponytail, I was then bused to Diamond Head Crater. The tour included a forty-five-minute hike to the top. Here we walked through a narrow tunnel to climb a spiral staircase to the summit. The view from the top was spectacular. A beautiful panorama of Waikiki, it's emerald hills, and the azure waters of the Pacific Ocean.

Again, my entire body was aching by the time I returned to the hotel. My legs from the hike, and my arms from holding onto the Dolphins. Sean was in the lobby when I came in dragging my feet. "Do I get to tie you up again tonight?" He whispered after he changed direction to intercept me.

"Only if it leads to you massaging my feet and legs." I put my head on his shoulder pretending to sleep. "Maybe my arms too, and my back, and head, and bum."

"Have you stretched?" Sean asked, moving me away to arms distance, then he turned and walked me to the path that led down to the cottages.

"Not yet. I'll do some yoga before my shower."

"Don't come back up for dinner. Just order room service when you are ready."

"Are you sure?" Not that I objected to the idea, I loved it. I just didn't want to miss spending time with him.

"Go rest," Sean smiled. "I'll see you when I get home." He kissed the crown of my head and gave me a covert smack on the bum to send me on the way.

At the cottage, I stripped down to my swimmers, and stepped out onto the white sand in front of Sean's place. Moving through a yoga sequence, I held positions longer to get a more effective stretch.

By the time I finished, I was able to sit and watch the blue disappear from the sky. The daylight washed away by currents of pink, red, orange, and purple, before shifting into the deep blue of tropical twilight.

Finishing my open-eyed meditation, I took myself inside and showered. I already felt more mobile, but the hot shower left me feeling alive again. I left my towel in the bathroom intending to dress and order something to eat, but I only made it as far as the bed.

I woke up to total darkness outside, but the light on in the kitchen. "Sean?" I called, hearing movement out in the lounge room. "God, please let it be Sean," I prayed quietly to myself.

"You're awake?" Sean smiled coming into the room. He was bare chested, just his pants slung low on his hips.

"I fell asleep," I yawned and looked at the clock. It was nearly eleven.

Sean dropped his pants, causing my breath to catch at the sight of him naked. I squirmed in reaction. The bed dipped under Sean's weight and he settled himself above me. "You did, but I needed the time to make some preparations for tomorrow anyway." Sean rubbed my nose with his playfully. "Do you still want that massage?" He ducked his head to my neck and pinched along my carotid.

"I think I'm okay, but I won't say no to a rub down," I breathed.

Sean smiled and moved his hand between my legs. "I could rub down here?"

"Perfect," I moaned and opened my legs for him.

Cassidy

A phone started ringing. I groaned. Sean looked over at the display. "I'll call him back," Sean assured, then he disappeared between my legs.

CHAPTER ELEVEN

"Dad, you called?" Sean spoke on the phone after we'd both cleaned up and showered. "When?" Sean got up and went into the kitchen. "Can you come a couple of days later? I'm going to be away."

I packed up my things while he spoke to his dad arranging dates and times for his visit. It didn't take me long to pack my clothes for the next two weeks of island hopping. Since Sean was still on the phone, I called Trish.

"Aren't you on a boat?" She answered.

"I didn't go on the cruise. I was ready to kill one of my sisters and decided to stay in Hawaii and see more of it."

"Sadie?"

"How'd you guess?"

"Because she's always needed to bring you down to try and make herself feel better about herself. Probably stems from being the former whore in the family."

"Probably."

"So, when will you be back?"

"Not for a couple of weeks. I'm island hopping for the next two weeks, so I might be out of contact at times," I explained. "If you need to get hold of me, just email me."

"Oh, okay," Trish waited a minute. "Send me a photo of him when you hang up."

"Who?"

Trish laughed. "The guy who you stayed behind for."

"How could you possibly know?"

"Come on, how long have we been friends? As if I don't know your 'I met a guy' voice by now. How do you think I knew about Benjamin? Prick. So, who is he?"

"The manager of the hotel we were staying in."

"When they say girls have a type...," Trish teased. "So, is he a worthwhile rebound?"

"Started out rebound, is now a holiday fling."

"Oh god!"

"What?" I asked, worried something had happened.

"Holly, you went away to get over a broken heart, not to break it twice."

"I wasn't in love with Benjamin."

"And I'm a white chick with a skinny arse from England."

Trish was South American. She had a gorgeous figure, despite her focus on her arse, it wasn't sizable. Air hostesses' uniforms only went to a certain size to encourage them to stay svelte. Trish could gain twenty pounds and still wear her work dress.

"You're hot, and you know it. At least you can tan."

"You missed my point."

"No, I ignored it." Sean walked back into the room. He sat on the end of the bed and started massaging one of my feet.

"Just keep reminding yourself it's only sex."

"Only sex. Right. Got it." I winked at Sean. "You have to stop doing that," I told him, "Trish tells me I'm only allowed to use you for sex."

"Just sex?" Sean smirked. "What about tour guide?"

"I'll ask."

"Oh my god," Trish groaned. "It's too late. I'll start preparing the broken heart recovery party now."

"You are such a pessimist," I teased.

"Holly, he lives there, you live here, you must know it's never going to work out?"

"Three weeks, Trish," I assured. "I'll be home in three weeks."

"Sure." Trish hung up.

"Another sister?" Sean asked.

"Flatmate and best friend," I advised. "Your dad is coming

to visit?"

"Yeah," Sean frowned a little. "His visit will cross over with your being here, but I've explained I'll be busy and he'll have to enjoy my company on occasion until I go back to work."

"You didn't tell your dad about me?"

Sean smirked. "He guessed I had a woman. I told him I'd let him meet you if he promised to be on good behavior."

Taking my foot out of his grasp, I squirmed a little. "Do you think I should? I mean, I'll be leaving a few days after he gets here, so what's the point?"

"I guess the point would be to be polite. It's two weeks away, Holly, there is a lot of room for growth in that time."

"Growth into what?" I asked confused. Sean stood up, putting his back to me as he stacked our two bags by the door. "Sean, this is a holiday fling. I have a job and life to go back to in Australia. I can't afford to become emotionally invested in a guy who lives ten hours away by plane. Hell, I can't afford the commute to be able to see you on a regular basis. This thing would fizzle and die for you before I even set foot on the Tarmac in Sydney."

"Do you know the biggest problem with our jobs, Holly?" Sean huffed.

I frowned, confused by the change of topic. "No."

"We are always anticipating problems and trying to prevent them, or solve them ahead of time." Sean came back to the bed. "We tend to forget that you can't do that with everything, and relationships is one of those things. You are very good at your job, Holly. I saw that the day we met with the way you solved your room issue. I've seen it in the way you observe my staff and what happens at my hotel." He smiled sadly. "You suck at relationships, and now I know why."

"I do not suck at them. The guys I date fuck them up, just like you are doing by acting like this is one when we agreed it wasn't."

"I agreed to see where this went," Sean clarified. He moved forward on the bed, to be hovering in front of me.

Cassidy

"I can't, Sean. I'm just getting over being fucked over by a guy. I can't…"

"Holly!" Sean snapped calmly. "Stop over analyzing the situation. We enjoy each other's company. You promised me three weeks. Let's take this as it comes."

I met his eyes, thrown by how intent they were on me. "If you make me fall in love with you, I'm going to hate you for it."

Sean caressed my face. "If you make me fall in love with you and leave me, I'm going to come find you, Holly."

"No, you won't."

Sean smiled. "You're right because if I fall in love with you, I'm never going to let you go." He kissed me before I could respond, forcing me back on the bed beneath him.

He kissed me, taking my mind off our different opinions, and tuning it into something more real. Like his firm body pressing mine to his bed. My hands crept across his back and shoulders, tangling my fingers in his hair.

Sean's phone started ringing again. Sean broke away from the kiss and looked at the screen. "Hold that thought," he excused answering the phone. "Dad?" Sean slipped his hand beneath my top to caress me. "Can you email that to me? Will see you then." Sean hung up. "Now, what were we talking about?"

"Fucking," I answered. "Definitely fucking."

CHAPTER TWELVE

The early dawn found us boarding a decent sized motorized yacht. "It's mine, and I rent it out for guests to use," Sean explained as we stowed our bags in the bedroom.

"Do I need to use a fluoroscope to check the bed?"

Sean smiled. "It gets professionally cleaned after each hire. It's our home for the next two weeks," he informed me and went back upstairs to the cockpit.

Stowing my gear, I followed him up as he started the engine. "Can I help?"

"Release the lines."

"Um, before I do that," I hesitated. "Do I keep the ropes, or leave them on the jetty?"

Sean chuckled and took me to the first line, showing me how to do it properly. "You get the one at the port bow," Sean directed. I stood there blinking at him. Sean smirked and pointed as he headed back to the cockpit. "Front of the boat."

Releasing the line by myself, I coiled the rope as he had done, then made my way to the cockpit. Sean was already motoring us out from the mooring and carefully past the reef. Once we were out a bit, Sean moved the stick - which I was guessing was the throttle or accelerator - forward. We started speeding through the water north.

"Why not fly?"

"By the time we drove to the airport, caught a charter to the island, drove to another hotel and checked in, we'll be there. Besides, this way we come and go on our timetable, not the airlines." Sean hesitated for a second. "You don't get motion sickness, do you?"

"No, I love boats."

Placing his arm around my waist, Sean pulled me close to him. He kissed me tenderly. His eyes hungry when he pulled away. "I should have hired a skipper," he sighed. "I could have spent time below deck ravishing you."

"You could teach me to drive instead," I suggested. "That way if you get pulled overboard by a shark, I can escape."

Sean looked at me bewildered. "Pulled overboard by a shark?"

"Yeah."

"Does that often happen in your country?" Sean chuckled.

"More than you want to know. Especially when couples go out alone together on the eve of one applying for a divorce."

"Ah, I see."

"I don't think you do," I corrected as he moved my body in front of his and placed my hands on the wheel. "I come from a country where every animal wants to kill you. All the fauna is deadly. Psychopaths creeping through bush, sea, and your own home in some cases."

Sean put his hands around my waist. "That's right, world's most deadly spiders and snakes, right?"

"Don't forget Kangaroos, Koalas, platypus, sea snakes, blue ring octopus, white pointers, bull sharks - who come into the fresh water - crocodiles, and the drop bears are the worst."

"Drop bears?"

"The worst! The number of campers killed by those... I was terrified of tents as a child by the time my brothers got through warning me about drop bears."

"You're pulling my leg, right?" Sean chuckled. "I mean, don't you ride kangaroos to school as kids?"

"Oh, yeah, sure, but you wouldn't approach someone else's kangaroo. Especially not a wild one. They have claws longer than my hand and can gut someone. Koalas are just as dangerous. We have professionals whose sole job is to keep them off the harbor bridge and opera house. Little bastards climb all over the city buildings and take chunks out of them. They leave huge gouges in the glass and stone. Very dangerous if they get you alone after dark."

Sean was quiet behind me for a moment. I was struggling to keep the smile off my face and my voice serious.

"You know I'm looking this up when we reach port right?" Sean whispered in my ear. "If you are bullshitting me, I'm going to spank you till your bum cheeks match the sunset."

I squirmed against him. "Now I wish I'd lied and told you they were cute and cuddly."

Sean's fingers gripped my waist as his body reacted to my bum rubbing against his groin. "Lord, have mercy. Let's focus on you driving the boat."

Sean taught me to slow the boat, stop it, and start it again during the three hours to the island Kauai. Our first stop was the Wailua Marina where we were only stopping for the afternoon. We joined the afternoon kayak tour to secret falls. Sean and I shared a tandem kayak up the Wailua River. He sat in the back as the strongest of us and insisted on taking photos of me paddling. He also started a water fight with me halfway up the river by 'accidentally' splashing me.

We left the kayaks and hiked to secret falls where we swam beneath the fall with the rest of the group. Sean and I frolicking and flirting like horny teenagers. By the time we returned to our boat, it was approaching sunset. We cruised down to Lihue and docked there for the night.

We ate dinner on the wharf before taking an evening stroll along the coastline. "We have an early morning tomorrow," Sean murmured in my ear as we lay intertwined in bed later. "We should think about sleeping."

I panted something like yes, before Sean gently circled his hips again. We were both covered in sweat, enjoying a slow, intimate session. Sean was taking his sweet time, making me praise him and God repeatedly for the last hour or so.

Sean's smile beamed in the low light of our cabin. "I want

to cum, but I'm enjoying being here, inside of you too much."

It had been a long day, but I knew exactly what he meant. "I want you to sleep inside me. I want you to cum, then put it back inside me bare, and sleep there."

Sean closed his eyes, Adam's apple bobbing, neck muscles straining. Sucking his earlobe into my mouth, I bit down a little till he groaned and thrust deeper. I smiled releasing his ear. "Pin me down and fuck me, Sean."

Needing no further encouragement, Sean pinned my hands above my head and pounded me hard and deep. I was breathless, pleasure racking my body, making me arch and beg for him to fill me with his cum.

Sean obliged me, growing significantly in girth, my eyes bulging at the feel as he hammered me. A moment later Sean cried out, his hips jolting with each heaving spurt of climax. It felt amazing, so much so, that my own body reacted and I came for him again.

Holding himself trembling above me, Sean opened his eyes and looked down at me. His eyes glittered in the night, thoughts racing. I could see it, see that he wanted to say something to me. My own heart was beating double time. "That was amazing."

Sean smiled, dropped a kiss to my lips and he fell beside me breathless. He went to the bathroom, then came back and snuggled in behind me. "I washed," he soothed as he slid his still semi-hard cock back inside me and wrapped me in his arms.

I didn't care. I was on birth control, and I believed Sean when he told me he was clean. It would do no physical harm. "Did you use condoms with her," I asked half asleep.

"I loved her," he replied, casually, as if that answered everything.

It made me think about that sentiment and what it meant to me. Was I in love with Benjamin? Was that why I was happy to forgo protection with him? I know condoms didn't mean anything to him but an inconvenience. I was so caught up in his interest in me, it hadn't bothered me.

I'd only been with my fiancé before Benjamin, and we used protection out of my fear of getting knocked up. "I've only had unprotected sex with Ben," I whispered. "That doesn't mean I loved him."

Sean's breathing, which had been heavy, changed for a moment. His arm tightened his hold on me. "I only claim what I intend to keep." I frowned at his words, not awake enough to process it.

"Get some sleep, Holly," he urged. The kiss on my shoulder made me smile. Bare naked sex didn't mean love to me, but Sean's kisses were starting to mean something.

CHAPTER THIRTEEN

At ten the next morning we were on tour in the Kauai backcountry on a zip line adventure. We flew above the lush tropical rainforest canopy, zipped across valleys and gullies, and soared over streams.

We followed that up with a trip to the enchanting Hali'i waterfall to enjoy a picnic lunch and swim. We'd found a space of our own beside the tiered waterfall, enjoying a walk through the rainforest to get there. We sat watching the splendor of the falls and just enjoying being with each other. "Hali'i, in Hawaiian, means to cover like a blanket," Sean murmured as he covered my body with his on the bank.

I smiled up at him as he moved his hand down my waist to shift the gusset of my swimsuit aside. "Is this an appropriate place?"

Sean smiled as he unzipped himself, eyes looking around to make sure we were still alone. "It's a magnificent place."

He kissed my mouth heatedly as he pressed into me. I gasped feeling how turned on he was. Lifting my hips, I encouraged both of us to get there sooner. Any of the others on tour could decide a walk in the rainforest would be good.

I couldn't believe that the sex with Sean just kept on getting better and better each day. When my body tightened with delight, I bit Sean's shoulder to prevent anyone else hearing me find paradise.

Sean grunted in my ear and quickly pulled back, letting his release fertilize the earth. Sitting up, I righted my clothing and watched his seed soak into the soil. "You just seeded the earth," I teased.

Sean grinned fixing himself up and collapsed into my lap. "Next time we come here, there might be a tree with juicy, delicious fruit on it."

I laughed. "It will be rather popular, possibly the world's best aphrodisiac."

Sean lifted a brow. "World's best?"

I blushed. "Well, the best in my world, so far."

"Hmm. I might have to up my game, ensure I keep the world's best title for the rest of your days."

I smiled at him. He smiled back, caressing my cheek. "You blush so easily, Holly."

"Its new for me. You started it."

The happiness reached Sean's eyes as he pulled my mouth to his. "So, you blush only for me."

"You have that effect on me."

Something serious flashed in Sean's eyes as he brushed his lips over mine. He pulled me to him, and I went willingly. Lying in his arms, kissing in paradise.

That afternoon, we took our last walk through Lihue. We enjoyed a casual meal before retiring to the yacht for the night. Watching a movie in each other's arms, we fell asleep much the same way.

Sean woke me early in the morning, his body hard and eager for me. I knew I was going to miss this when I went home, but it was an experience I needed.

"You need to stop lying there grinning and get ready for the day. Our tour leaves at nine," Sean teased as he stepped out of the shower with just a towel around him.

Eying him up, I grabbed the towel pulling him onto the bed. "That's still plenty of time for more of you."

Sean laughed as he covered my body with his. The towel flung across the room as he gave me a second helping of holiday lust. I was giddy and grinning madly as we raced to the tour office, barely making our ride.

After being fitted with gloves, a helmet and headlamp, we climbed into a four-wheel drive and headed inland. We crossed old sugar cane fields as the guide explained the history of the plantation.

"Around eighteen seventy a series of ditches were hand-dug by Chinese laborers to deliver water from the rainforest to the sugar cane fields. This land is privately owned and only recently been accessible to the public after the closure of the plantation," the guide educated us. He then went on to tell us about the lives of the workers.

The car stopped for a photo op at a lookout that gave the best view of Waialeale Crater away from a helicopter tour. A few minutes later, we arrived at the start of the narrow man-made channel and provided with a safety demonstration.

"It's a pity we can't share," Sean whispered before he climbed into his tube and prepared for the ride.

"I could sit on your lap the entire way, but I'm worried it could get dangerous."

"True, the spectators may get jealous." Sean's eyes went to the group of young men standing in line. I smiled shaking my head and dropping into my tube.

It was a cross between mild white water rafting and a lazy river ride. The water was knee deep in most places, and the current moved us along fast enough that no paddling was required.

Every opportunity Sean could, he caught my hand and held it. We floated in and out of tunnels, one of which was almost one and a half kilometers long. We glided hand in hand with only dim headlamps to light our way through. My fear of never emerging was only dampened by Sean's hand in mine.

At the end of the tubing adventure, the guides served up a picnic lunch at a beautiful, natural swimming hole. Sean and I sat hand in hand while we ate, then we splashed and hugged as we swam with the other tourists.

On the way back to the tour office, we sat side by side. My head rested on Sean's muscular chest, his arm firmly around my shoulders. "Thank you for insisting I stay." Smiling, I linked fingers with his free hand. "It's already been an experience I won't soon forget."

Sean kissed the top of my head, his arm wrapping me

tighter to him. He didn't need to say anything in response. I found the silence between us to be more comfortable then I could ever imagine.

Returning to the boat after lunchtime, we headed to our next destination. The far side of the Kauai island. We arrived at the Na Pali coast in the late afternoon. The sun casting a dramatic light upon the majestic cliffs.

"It's considered to be the Jewel of Kauai." Sean wrapping me in his arms as we observed the breathtaking beauty of it.

"I can see why."

"Those cliffs are close to three thousand feet."

"I live in the metric world," I teased. Lifting my camera, I stepped free to take photos.

Sean steered the boat while I took photos of the green valleys, hidden beaches, and magnificent secluded waterfalls that dropped from hanging valleys into the ocean below. It was absolutely breathtaking.

"I want to get a photo of you," I told Sean.

Stopping the boat, he came to me. "You can have one of the both of us." He took the camera and held it away from us as he took me in his arms. Taking out my phone, I connected remotely to the camera to line up the shot then posed and tapped my screen to take the photo. The camera clicked.

"Keep tapping," Sean whispered as he turned his face to mine and kissed me.

When he pulled back, I knew my happiness was shining out from my insides. It was the happiest I could ever remember being.

We ate dinner on the deck watching the sun begin to set. Before it became too dark, Sean took to the wheel and cruised us toward our destination for the night. Twenty minutes south.

That night, the heat between us was remarkable. Sean took me slow and deep, making me wait for my release. Every touch and kiss was intense. I had to believe it was an enchantment of this place, this paradise on earth.

I fell asleep in Sean's arms, drawing randomly through the sheen of perspiration on his skin. We both needed showers but couldn't bear to disturb what just happened between us.

"I wish this holiday never had to end," I whispered when his breathing grew heavy. "I've never had a more perfect week than this."

*****

"Sean," a deep voice called as heavy footsteps thumped above deck. "Cassidy, you in there?" A big fist thumped on the hatch above the room.

Sean muttered a curse and rolled out of bed pulling his shorts on as the banging started again. "Give it a break, Tama. I'm not alone."

"Crap, sorry, Sean."

Sean opened the door and made his way above deck while I grumbled and tried to find my clothes with my eyes closed. I finally managed to pull knickers and a dress on, then went to find out if we were being pirated or something.

As I came above deck, I blinked into the early dawn light. Sean stood at the back of the boat talking to a man twice his breadth and of Polynesian descent. He was bulk muscle and the sort of guy if you met in the dark, you'd wet yourself.

His eyes came to me over Sean's shoulder, and his lips pulled up on one side. "Girlfriend?" The man tilted his head towards me.

Sean turned and put his arm out towards me. "Not yet. Tama, meet Holly, she's on holiday, and I'm showing her the best of Hawaii."

"And you brought her to meet me. I'm flattered," Tama smiled and pulled me into a hug. "It's nice to meet you, Holly. Where do you come from?"

"Australia," I muffled a yawn. Sean smirked and tucked me into his side to kiss the top of my head.

"Australia?" Tama's brows jumped. "Well, that's a bit away."

"Holly is in the hotel business as well," Sean informed his friend. "Tama runs my resort and tour company here in Waimea."

I felt my brows lift but didn't comment on the news that he owned more than one resort. "And he's here at the crack of dawn to give you his report?" I grumbled instead.

Tama chuckled. "Business happens via email. No, I heard Sean was on holiday and saw the yacht moored here. I thought I'd drag Sean out for a spot of fishing. Do you like fishing, Holly?"

"Not as much as I like sleeping, Tama," I tried to hide another yawn.

Sean's body shook with restrained laughter beside me. "I might pass, Tama. I'm taking Holly to Ni'ihau in a few hours for snorkeling and then heading back to O'ahu for the night before continuing to Maui."

"Will you be stopping in Moloka'i?" Tama lifted a curious brow.

Sean shrugged a shoulder. "We'll spend a couple of days there before we head back."

Sean's answer surprised Tama. He looked me over this time, from head to toe. "Well, I won't keep you. You're going to be traveling a fair distance the next few days. Promise me you'll visit again soon for a fish."

Sean smiled. "I'll be here for our usual catch up."

Tama smiled at me. "Will you be joining us on that visit, Holly?"

I shook my head. "No, I'm heading home in a little over two weeks."

Tama looked to Sean whose mouth lifted on one side like I'd told a cute joke. Tama shook his head. "Well, it was nice meeting you, Holly. Keep your eyes open on the crossing to the island. There are lots of dolphins and whales this time of year. I'll see you in three weeks, Sean."

Tama left us shaking his head and laughing softly to himself. Sean turned me to him and kissed me. The kiss was gentle and tentative. When Sean pulled back, there was a crease in his brows. I used my thumb to iron it out. "Something wrong?"

Sean inhaled deeply. "Last night, the two of us."

I smiled. "That was pretty intense. Those cliffs definitely had an effect."

"Oh, it was the cliffs?" Sean queried humored.

"Absolutely. I'd say it was the best sex of my life." I stopped and thought about it. "Yep, definitely the best. I doubt you could repeat or improve upon last night."

"I believe that's a challenge, Miss Claire."

I smirked backing up. "Oh, you think you could top that?"

"Absolutely." Sean stalked towards me. His eyes twinkled.

I squeaked and ran below deck for the cabin. Sean was right behind me. He tackled me in the narrow aisle and pinned me to the wall. His hands were under my dress relieving me of my underwear, his mouth searching mine for submission.

My hands shoved Sean's shorts to the floor; then I pressed my feet against the opposite wall to lift myself for him. Sean groaned as I slipped him between my folds and he found my moist core.

Sean pulled back, tilting my face so I could look down into his lust filled eyes. "You make me wild for you, Holly. Make me want to throw caution to the wind, to lose control, but I hate not cumming in you."

I bit my lip at the hunger in his eyes. He searched my face, looking for an answer to a secret question. I forced his mouth to mine and kissed him heatedly. Sean moaned and gripped my bum. He turned towards the cabin, holding me above him as he walked.

In the cabin, he dropped me on the bed and quickly collected a condom while I yanked my dress over my head. Sean crawled into the bed with me, his hunger raw in his eyes. I knew what he wanted, but as I turned to lay on my stomach and lift my hips for him, I worried there was more to his hunger than lust.

As he pressed me into the bed, I gripped the sheets and closed my eyes. There was something between Sean and I that went beyond physical desire. I knew that from the moment we met. I thought it was like what I had with Benjamin, but as I thought back, I realized, it had always been more than that.

"Fuck," I moaned, realizing I was entering dangerous

waters with Sean, but I couldn't walk away now. I didn't want to. I wanted my three weeks of paradise. My heart would need to barricade itself against anything more. My head and body needed this.

Sean circled his hips inward, plunging into my depths, reaching for a part of me I couldn't risk him reaching. I whimpered and moaned, wondering if he was already farther in than I knew.

My body seized on the awareness, and I cried out helpless, surrendering my body to the effect Sean had on me. As we lay panting, I buried my face in the pillow and cursed at myself. Suddenly, that three-week deadline couldn't come fast enough and was too soon all at once.

Huffing, I sagged into the mattress. I wasn't going to give up my dream job for a man I met on holiday. I was determined. Sex and fun. That's all this could be. No matter what, I was going home at the end of three weeks.

CHAPTER FOURTEEN

"Where are we going?" I asked Sean as he carried my bag away from the boat.

"It's a surprise."

Smiling, I walked beside him to the road where a taxi was waiting. "If I remember correctly, the itinerary stated today and tomorrow were Molokai. But it didn't state what we were doing here."

"You sound suspicious."

"I am. I'm ready to bum around on the beach and read a book. This island looks like the hiking and extreme sports kind of place."

Sean held the door for me to hop in the taxi. He caught my mouth as I stepped up to him. "It's a surprise."

Taking the hint, I enjoyed the scenic drive from the harbor around the shore and up into the mountains. The taxi dropped us at a cottage and Sean led the way inside. Buggered - not in the sodomized sense, just tired - I followed. So far, we'd spent every day on all the adventure tours I wanted to do, plus extra that Sean declared necessary. There was nothing left on my list to do.

I walked through the neatly decorated cottage to the back deck. This part of the cottage sat on poles over the forest canopy below. In awe, I stepped outside and took in the view. Across the ocean, I could see a city skyline on a distant shore. "Is that Maui?"

"Sure, is." Sean wrapped his arms around me from behind. "Beautiful isn't it?"

"Not even close to the right adjective," I breathed.

"This is my place here. My hide away from the world. I've always come here alone. But, this time, I wanted to bring you here, Holly." Flattered, I gazed out into the distance, still in awe of the raw natural beauty before me. "Holly, I've grown to like you very much these past few weeks. I'd like you to consider staying longer."

Frowning, coming back to the here and now, I tried to comprehend what Sean was asking. "I thought we were staying two nights? Don't you have to get back to your dad?"

Sean turned me to face him, keeping me close. "We are, and we can come back here whenever you want, if you stay. Don't go home, yet."

My mouth moved, my brain scrambling to find something to say. Nothing came out.

"I know I'm asking a lot, but there is something more than a fling between us, Holly. Something worth pursuing long term." Sean swept my hair back from my face. "Don't answer today. We have two days here with nothing to distract us, and stuck in each other's pocket. What I'd like you to keep in the back of your mind, is if you want to leave without exploring what could be us."

I took a deep breath. Sean pressed his finger to my lips. "I said don't answer today. Just keep the idea in the back of your mind."

Waiting till Sean took his finger away, I licked my lips and nodded. I'd think about it, but I knew my answer. Sean smiled. "I'll go unpack our bags and make us some lunch."

"You have food here?".

"I have a housekeeper. She stocks the fridge for me when I let her know I'm coming."

"So, what is our plan for the rest of the day?" I asked, following him back inside.

"No plans. The next two days are carefree us time."

"Huh," I replied nonchalantly. I lifted myself to sit on the kitchen counter. "So, if I just want to lay around reading?"

Sean lifted a brow. "I have a few books to read too. Happy to lay around with you."

*****

I woke up in Sean's arms two mornings later. Sean's question front and center of my mind. To say the last two days were bliss would be an understatement. Sean and I seemed to fit without either of us trying. We sat around reading; we were intimate, we cooked and laughed together as we got to know each other better.

We would be leaving this place of peace today to return to Oahu and life. These two days were going to stay entrenched in my memory for the rest of my life above any other over the last two weeks. The moment where my eyes fluttered open, my heart rippled in the happiness of the moment, and I realized I was in love.

I wanted to forehead slap myself, but I couldn't get the smile off my face. It was a collision of happiness and misery, and neither emotion was willing to give an inch. I was flying home in four days. Home. To my friends and the job, I'd always aspired to have. But, to leave meant I gave up the best relationship of my life. Sean could be the one. Could I walk away from him, board a plane, and continue with my life without regretting it?

It was the fork in the road. The one people always remembered. The choice of two futures, either choice you win and lose. My career, or love? Could it remain heaven? I wasn't stupid enough to think that there wouldn't be ups and downs, but it could be close to perfect.

As if hearing my thoughts, Sean woke up, or, a very hard part of him woke and tapped my bum cheek. By the time I rolled to face him, Sean's eyes were open, his mouth smiling at me. His eyes observed mine, and for a moment he hesitated. He searched my eyes, and then a smile bloomed across his face.

"It will be worth it, Holly." His mouth brushed mine, his hand skimmed over my waist. "I'll make a few calls about jobs that are available for you when I get back today. That way, you'll know the opportunity you are giving up to be with me, will still exist with me."

"I'm considering it; it's not set in stone, Sean. I'll still need to go home and get my stuff, and I can't just leave Trisha high and dry."

Sean pulled me closer. "I'll come with you. I've always wanted to visit Australia."

"You want to make sure I don't change my mind once I get home," I teased.

"It's a hard decision to make, Holly. I understand what you are giving up to try being with me. I also know how influential friends can be. They talk you into sense out of fear, rather than following your heart."

"Don't make me regret this, Sean. Tell me anything now you think may be a problem for us?"

Sean opened his mouth just as his phone started ringing. The curse that came out directed at his phone was impressive. "Hello?" He answered rolling away. "What happened?" Sean scrubbed his hand through his hair while he listened. "Damn it! Okay. I'll call and organize a car. I'll be back at the resort by nine and will sort that out when I get there."

Sean hung up his phone and turned to look at me. "Work could be a problem. Then there is my father."

"What about him?"

Sean sighed. "You'll understand when you meet him, which, is going to be sooner than later. He's landed at the airport, five hours earlier than expected and I need to organize a car to collect him since I'd booked one for later. We need to get back. Two weeks without a major incident was asking too much."

"Another celebrity?" I asked climbing out of bed.

"Cheating spouse. Got busted by the other partner and the husband threw punches at the other guy," Sean explained. "Unfortunately, that other guy is one of my employees."

"Ouch!"

"Tell me about it. The police are there. Just the sort of shit I needed." Sean scrubbed his head again and started scrolling his phone for a number. "You shower first. I'll join you once I've at least got one problem sorted."

An hour later we arrived at the marina and boarded Sean's

boat. It took us a little over two hours to get back to the Cassidy resort. We took our luggage back to Sean's and then Sean left me there to deal with his business. I started looking into visa applications.

After realizing what a pain moving to Hawaii was going to be just in getting a visa. I sighed and collapsed on the lounge. I found my phone and called home. Trisha didn't answer, telling me she was either asleep or working. "Hey, you're going to hate me. Sean's asked me to stay longer, and I think I want to try. I've never connected with a guy like this. What if I never meet another guy who gets me like this one? It's worth trying, isn't it? I'll speak with you soon. Love you."

With nothing else to do, I changed, grabbed Sean's board and went for a surf. The weather wasn't fantastic. The waves were breaking a bit close to shore, but I still managed to enjoy myself. We'd had some rain while away. Sean wouldn't let that stop us from doing whatever he planned that day. Every day for the past two and a half weeks had been fantastic.

By lunchtime, I showered and dressed and was back to trying to work out the logistics of moving my life to Hawaii. This time, I was on the phone to the American consulate about the best visa for which I could apply. Sean came home and sat beside me, looking over all the information I'd scribbled down on a notepad. "Okay, thank you," I hung up.

"That's rather a heavy sigh?" Sean smirked.

"I think you'll have to find someone to run your resort and move to Australia to keep dating me. Fewer hoops to jump through." Pushing the list of what he would have to do to move to Australia next to the one for me to move here.

"You looked up what I needed to do?" Sean chuckled. "Well, at least I know you are serious about being with me, and it's not the venue making this decision for you."

"Absolutely not. Beautiful as it is here, I love my country." I pushed the lists away. "Has your dad arrived?"

"Yes. He's settling into his room."

"And the police?"

"Sorted. The guests involved have left, albeit separately. My former employee has decided not to press charges and resigned."

"You didn't fire him?"

"I would have. But, by resigning he gets paid out his leave. Since he was working while injured, his insurance will cover his medical fees."

"You gave him a choice, didn't you?"

"He assured me the affair occurred while he was off shift, but the man accosted him during his shift. It's fair." Sean took my hand and stood. "I'm not officially back at work, so we have the afternoon to ourselves. How about we go back to bed and wake up properly?"

Smirking, I stood, placing my bum on the table. "There is a perfectly good table right here."

Sean's lips twitched on the side. He moved between my thighs, arms wrapping around my waist. "I want to cum in you, Holly. The condoms are in the bedroom."

Butterflies took flight in my stomach. I met his ocean blue eyes, and I never wanted to stop staring at them. "We can start here, finish there."

Sean cupped my cheek in his hand. "We will start here and continue in the bedroom." His mouth brushed mine, his body moving forward to press me back on the table till he hovered over me. Staring into my eyes, his eyes became serious. "I never intend to finish with you, Holly."

CHAPTER FIFTEEN

"You look nervous," Sean smirked as he pulled my chair out for dinner.

"I'm about to meet your dad after knowing you for three weeks. It's insane."

"Relax, Holly. He's just my dad," Sean chuckled. "And if it helps, he met my mother one day and proposed the next. My father is a big believer in love at first sight."

My eyes watched Sean as he took the seat next to me. "Do you?"

"I wouldn't have sent you the dessert that first night if I didn't," Sean revealed. "You already twisted my arm into a suite with free breakfast. I own three resorts, Holly. I'm not usually that bad at business."

"You thought I was a porn star."

"Not when we first met. When I ran into you on the path, I was deep in thought wondering how I would handle it if you were. Thankfully, that wasn't the case. So, dessert." He winked at me. His eyes moved to the entry, and he stood again. I recognized his father walking towards us and rose as well.

"Sean," his dad grinned and hugged him.

"Dad, this is Holly Claire. Holly, my father Raymond Cassidy," Sean introduced.

I put my hand out. Raymond shook it firmly. "Lovely to meet you, Holly. Any relation to Nathan Claire?"

My tongue felt too big for my mouth. "Do you think Claire is that uncommon a surname in Australia?"

"Sean told me your father was in politics. I made the connection," Raymond defended politely.

"He's my father."

"Ah," Raymond looked intrigued. He took his seat, and I sat back down. "So, how long have you two been seeing each other?"

"Three weeks," Sean replied taking my hand in his. "Best three weeks of my life. So far."

"Do you live locally, Holly?"

"No, I am on holidays."

Raymond raised a brow. "Oh, when do you go home?"

"Sunday," I answered.

"And what do you do for work?" Raymond inquired.

"I'm effectively a general manager for a resort."

Raymond smiled. "So, you come here regularly to check in on the Hawaiian branch of your resort?"

My brows furrowed. "Ah, no. I was here on holiday with my sisters."

Raymond looked confused; he tilted his head in question at Sean. Sean put his hand over mine. "Holly stayed on three extra weeks to be with me. Her older sisters cruised back. I'm trying to convince Holly to stay on permanently."

"Oh, I see," Raymond smiled in relief. "And is he succeeding, Holly?"

"He was until I saw the criteria for my getting a visa. I've suggested Sean moving to Australia would be easier."

"You expect him to give up his life, everything he has built here to follow you?" Raymond accused.

I raised a brow. "If it didn't work out, Sean would still have his resorts here and return to his home. He would possibly gain by opening a new resort in Australia, giving his brand an overseas market. If I move here, I give up my dream job, my apartment, my friends and my life. If it doesn't work out, I've got nothing to go home to, Raymond. You think that is the fairer option?"

Raymond sat back. "I suppose not." Raymond looked at his son. "Are you considering moving to Australia?"

"No, dad. I couldn't return to a busy city lifestyle after ten years here. Currently, the plan is for Holly to relocate here. If visas become an issue, we will discuss other options then."

Raymond seemed satisfied with this answer and opened his menu to browse. Sean lifted my hand off the table and kissed my palm. When I met his eyes, he winked at me. "So, how are negotiations going for that place in Ko Olina?" Raymond asked.

"Stalled currently. I made an offer, but the owner is trying to get someone to outbid me. I've told them if they don't accept by Monday, I'll rescind my offer."

"Do you think they will take it?" Raymond raised a brow.

"If they don't, they will struggle to find someone who will offer even close to what I have and risk bankruptcy."

"Well, if that goes well, you could offer Holly your role here while you get the new resort operational."

Sean squeezed my hand gently. "Dad, you know I have a code about relationships with my staff. Holly also needs to have her independence. There are plenty of opportunities for her here."

Raymond turned to me with raised brows. "He's very headstrong, Holly. Are you sure you are capable of enduring him?"

"That's what we are going to find out, Raymond."

Raymond's eyes glinted. After we ordered our meals, Raymond turned his attention back to Sean. They discussed golf, the weather, the new president-elect, issues of state, and issues in Hawaiian politics. Truthfully, the political talk was getting the best of me by the time dessert came.

"Are you planning on relaxing while here, Raymond? Or are you like Sean and need to be doing something while the sun is up?"

The men laughed. "Well, you figured us out already," Raymond conceded. "I'm booked into the sunrise hike. Sean won't pass up his morning surf to come with me. Maybe you would like to make the trek with me, Holly?"

"Holly surfs with me in the morning, dad."

"She can do that anytime," Raymond objected. "I only make it over here once a year. She should spend time with me. Get to know the old bastard you're going to grow into."

"You look too young and fit for anyone to be calling you an old bastard, Raymond," I laughed. "And I'd love to do the Sunrise hike with you. You can start telling me all the embarrassing youth stories about Sean."

Raymond smiled. Sean shook his head, but his lips pulled up. He was happy I was making an effort. That night, when we got back to his place, he showed me how glad he was.

*****

The next morning found me hiking alongside Raymond and six others. The weather was muggy, and I was sticky with sweat by the time we reached the peak to watch the sunrise.

"Worth the effort?" Raymond inquired with a smile.

"Anything worth having, usually is," I murmured. Closing my eyes, the sun blanketed me in its golden rays. The group fell quiet as we all enjoyed the peace of the moment. That first impact of sunlight for the day was always magical for me. I couldn't explain why. It just was.

The sun lifted and released its hold on me. I felt energized. Opening my eyes, I found Raymond observing me with a smile. "Has Sean told you much about his mother?"

"Just that she died while he was young," I sympathized. "And, that you loved her a lot."

Raymond smiled. "More than life." He walked away from the group a little, so I followed. "I met her at a charity function when I was twenty-two. I had just started as a junior in my father's law firm, and she was the assistant event manager for the function. It was her first big gig, and she wanted to make an impression. That meant it had to go perfectly," Raymond reminisced.

"Did it all go to hell?".

Raymond guffawed. "With Beth at the helm? Not likely. That woman was as determined as they come. No, the night went without a glitch. I watched her all night. I admired the way she handled the staff, and how she solved major problems without incident. Especially, how damned beautiful she was."

Cassidy

Raymond turned his head to meet my eyes. "She wasn't what would be considered beautiful by today's standards. But in the sixties, she could outshine Marilyn Monroe."

I smiled, getting a picture of the woman. Raymond turned his eyes back to the sunset. "The night was over, and people starting to leave, when she came up to me. Collecting a champagne glass and sipping it she asked me my name." Raymond's eyes twinkled. "We chatted about the evening. Eventually, she huffed and asked if I thought I might ask her to dance before the band stopped playing. I did. We danced. Then I walked her to the bus stop for her to get home. The last bus was pulling away as we turned the corner."

"So, you offered her a ride home?" I asked trying to guess the story.

"God, no. I was drunk," Raymond admitted. "My father drummed the whole drink driving thing into us boys before it was even a thing."

"Rather pioneering," I complimented.

"No, I took her home with me," Raymond smirked. "She wasn't as easy as she was forward. We stayed out on the back patio talking all night. Our hopes and dreams, ambitions and hesitations, our desires and needs." Raymond turned to face me. "But it wasn't until the sun rose and shined upon her face, that I saw the real woman hidden beneath. She closed her eyes and absorbed the first rays of light. The true meaning of peace revealed itself to me at that moment."

"Ah," I smiled understanding. "You came on this hike to be with your wife."

Raymond chuckled. "I am always with her, Holly." He tapped his left chest. "She's always with me. There has been no other since that day. When she opened her eyes again, I got down on one knee and asked her to marry me. She smiled, looked at the time and told me she needed to get home."

"So, she didn't say yes?"

"Not immediately. I drove her home, and she introduced me to her dad. So, I did the proper thing and asked him for her hand. He had four daughters. He was glad to be rid of one," Raymond laughed.

"That's not so sweet as I was expecting."

Raymond met my eyes. "Back in those days, women were expected to keep house, Holly. Beth told me straight up she was keeping her career, and she did. She was punished for it when she got pregnant the first time, effectively told by her boss to go home and be a proper wife. It took her a year to get her career back on track after that, only for her to fall pregnant again." Raymond studied my eyes. "I was sure she would resent me, her sons, for making her dreams harder to reach, but she didn't. She loved her boys, and she loved showing everyone she could be a good wife and mother and still have her dreams too."

I looked out at the horizon. "You are telling me the sacrifice to be with Sean will be worth it."

Raymond's eyes sparkled. "Sean has my spirit and drive, but he has his mother's determination. If you love him, Holly. He will support your dreams, and do what he can to see you fulfill them. All he will ever ask is for your love and devotion."

"I'm not exactly a religious girl, Raymond. But, if it's fidelity you worry about, that's never been an issue. I am loyal for as long as he is."

Raymond nodded. "Good. Should we head back? I was thinking of a surf myself this morning."

"If you don't object, I'll join you."

Raymond was pleasantly surprised. "You don't have to hang out with me, Holly. Neither Sean nor I will think bad of you."

"Oh, trust me, I'm not doing this to be nice," I snickered. "I'm still waiting for all those embarrassing stories you promised last night."

Raymond chortled. "You're gorgeous. Okay, let's start with my favorite…"

Cassidy

CHAPTER SIXTEEN

Walking into the restaurant, I went up on my tippy toes to find my dinner companions. Raymond and Sean sat at Sean's usual table. Smiling, I made my way to join them. They were talking pretty intently and didn't notice me approach.

I was just a table away when Henry walked the opposite way. "Evening, Miss Claire."

"Evening, Henry."

Sean's head snapped up. "We'll discuss it later, dad," Sean ended their conversation. He stood, giving me a genuine smile and welcoming hug. His lips brushed my cheek, and he lingered a little as he inhaled my hair. "How did it go?" Sean inquired as I took the seat beside him.

"Good. It's only a maternity relief position, but it's twelve months of paid work, and they would be willing to sponsor me."

"So, you accepted the role?" Raymond asked enthusiastically.

"Well, no, they haven't offered it yet. Kerry said she would get back to me by tomorrow evening, so I have time to make arrangements before I fly home."

Raymond turned to Sean. "Are you flying out Sunday as well?"

"I can't. I've just taken two weeks of leave," Sean advised. "Holly is flying home alone. She will make arrangements from there, and once her visa is approved, I will fly over. We'll spend a week in Australia finalizing everything before we come home."

"Sounds like you have it all planned out. Hopefully, the visa won't take too long."

I forced a smile. One of the things I needed to take care of when I got home, was telling Roger I wasn't accepting my dream job. I had no hesitation moving country to be with Sean, but I hated the idea of giving up that position. Roger and Sammy were great, and I'd been looking forward to working with them.

"Everything okay, Holly?" Sean asked as his dad excused himself, answering his phone.

"Yeah, just haven't heard from Trisha. She normally gets back to me within two days." It had been three days since I left the message. I didn't want to arrive back to a tirade, or worse, a room full of my sisters and an intervention.

"Maybe she needs time to process the news?" Sean suggested.

"Possibly."

After dessert Raymond excused himself for the fifth phone call since I joined them. "Your dad is popular tonight," I queried Sean.

Sean nodded and threw his napkin on the table. "And it looks like I'm about to get as busy." I followed Sean's eyes to the doorway, where Henry was signaling Sean. Sean stood up, bending down to kiss my head. "I'll see you back home."

Taking his hand, I stopped him leaving. "I thought you weren't back at work until Monday?"

Sean gave me a frustrated look. Nearly every day since we got back, he'd spent hours disappearing to deal with work. "I'm sorry, Holly. This isn't just a job to me. It's my business." He squeezed my hand and walked off.

Looking around, I noticed Raymond had wandered out by the pool. Giving up, I placed my napkin on the table and made my way back to the cottage. Changing into exercise gear, I spent an hour doing a flowing vinyasa yoga on the beach.

When I came back inside, Sean still wasn't home. After showering, I checked my phone. I'd missed a call from

Trisha while I'd been on the beach.

"Are you insane?" Trisha answered when I called her back. "You've known the guy four weeks, Holly. Four weeks! You have taken this rebound thing too far. Now, listen to me. You need to say goodbye to his gorgeous arse, get on a plane, and come home."

I waited to make sure she finished. "I'm in love with him."

The silence stretched out. Finally, Trisha exhaled. "Well, damn! I guess I need to apply for a job with Hawaiian airlines. If you are moving your skinny white arse to paradise, so am I."

My mouth fell open. "Really?"

"Yes! And, we are going to live together. You are going to date this guy for a proper length of time. Then, when I deem it true love, he can propose. You'll have a proper engagement, wedding, etc., and then I will let you move in with him," Trisha lectured. "I'm not letting you rush into this, Holly. That heart of yours is too fragile for this spontaneous love shit. You need to step back a few meters, and do this thing properly."

"You're going to move to Hawaii with me?" I asked getting excited.

"Hell, yes! I meant what I said, Holly. We'll get our own place. Deal?"

My smile stretched across my face. "You are the bestest friend in the world. I am going to give you the biggest hug when I see you Monday."

"What time do you land?" Trisha asked, her happiness evident in her voice.

"Seven at night," I answered.

Trisha huffed. "I'll be halfway to New Zealand by then. I'll see you Tuesday morning, and we can work out all the details over breakfast."

"Sounds good to me." It was the best outcome. "Thank you for understanding, Trisha."

"Moving countries doesn't bother me, Holly. Sticking with the best friend I've ever had is important. Plus, I love Hawaii. Why wouldn't I want to live there?"

"Are you sure?"

"If you are sure you've fallen in love with this guy. Enough that you would give up everything to be with him. Then, it's an experience worth being in the front row to see. Besides, finding a guy in Sydney has been a massive fail for me. Maybe I'll have more luck over there."

Snickering, I asked Trisha about her life and guys. We laughed about the few dates she'd had while I'd been away, then said goodnight till Tuesday. With time to spare, I packed most of my bag, then jumped online looking for an idea about places Trisha and I could rent. If we were going to live here, it needed to be by the beach. Residing with Sean had spoiled me for morning surfs and afternoon beach yoga.

CHAPTER SEVENTEEN

Sean looked over his shoulder and smiled at me. Heat filling my cheeks, I focused on the track through the trees. Ensuring the horse's footing was sure on this track, was more important than how sexy Sean looked on a horse.

We were on our way to the waterfall Sean brought me to on what should have been my last day three weeks ago. We rode in silence. I'd fallen asleep before Sean came home last night. This morning, our interaction had been about affection, not talking.

We made our way down the steep, narrow trail until we reached the bottom and dismounted.

"You're happier today," Sean observed as I pulled my dress overhead.

"Trisha called. She's decided to move here with me, and we are going to live together."

"Wait, my place is only two bedrooms."

It made me laugh. "Trisha and I are getting our own place. She will support this madness but wants me to do it properly. So, dating and everything first." Sean looked unsettled. "What's wrong?"

Pulling me close to him, Sean's naked chest warm against my bare stomach made things clench down below. "I intended for you to be moving in with me, Holly. It doesn't make sense to get another place when you are spending most nights with me anyway."

"Because our work schedules will mean we only get to see

each other at night during the week?" I clarified.

"Basically, yes. We'll at least have weekends together."

"And what about Ko Olina? When you go there to ensure your new resort gets on its feet, you'll be staying there during the week for months, right? And if I'm here, already traveling over two hours to work and back each day?"

"Ko Olina is closer to Waikiki," Sean debated. "So, you can stay there with me, and it shortens your drive to work."

"Exactly," I smiled tapping his chest. "And it's only half an hour from the airport for Trisha. I was looking at this last night, as well as places to rent. My thinking is that Trisha and I will get a place near Ko Olina. You can stay with me during the week when you are working on the new resort, and I can come North with you for weekends."

Sean didn't seem to like that idea. "What happens when I'm not at the west coast resort for the week?"

"I have to drive further to see you a couple of nights a week." With a shrug, I moved towards the water.

"Only a couple?"

"We can't live in each other's pocket, Sean. We need time out from each other, time with friends, time alone to process things. Trisha is right," I breathed, feeling more at ease with this plan. "We need to do this right. We need to date, get to know each other over the long term, not the short-term intense passion of something new."

Sean turned me to face him. "This isn't going to wane for me, Holly. I already know you are the love of my life. But, you're right. Slow and steady is best. So, if it makes you happier to find your own place, and for us to date, I'm okay with that." My smile beamed up at him. His eyes sparkled as his hand dropped to take mine. "But I don't want to wait years for you to be my wife, Holly." Sean dug something out of his pocket and dropped to one knee. "We can have a year-long engagement, a traditional length. But I want everyone to know you are going to be my wife."

Sean produced a beautiful diamond ring. My breath rushed out of my chest, my stomach clenched and my eyes pricked with tears.

"Take this ring as my promise that I will marry you, Holly. That I will be your loving husband, and my oath to always be there for you, in whatever way you need me. Let me plan my future, my family, with you."

"Sean!" I exhaled, a tear escaping.

"Will you be my wife, Holly? Will you promise to reserve the job of devoted husband for me only?"

I couldn't say no. I didn't want to. I knew Sean and I would work. "No sooner than a year?"

With a smirk, Sean slipped the ring on my finger. "As long as you need. All I ask is that you promise to come back to me."

"I will," I smiled through unshed tears. Trisha was going to flip.

Rising to standing, Sean embraced me. We kissed heatedly, the passion building. Sean dropped his mouth to my ear. "How about a skinny dip?"

Chuckling, I stepped back from him. Sean's grin lit up his face as I pulled the tie on my bikini top and tossed it aside. Sean opened his boardshorts and dropped them to the ground, his body hard and beautiful to observe. Hooking my thumbs on the side of my bottoms, I pushed them down. Sean's pupils dilated.

"Catch me," I challenged. I dove into the clear waters. Sean's splash sounded while I was still under the water, swimming towards the fall. Catching my ankle, he dragged me back through the water to him.

Surfacing, I caught a breath only to have him steal it away with the intensity of his kiss. Wrapping my thighs around his waist, I held tight as Sean moved us to the rocky outcrop near the base of the falls. The spray of water showered us as my back pressed against the stone. Sean using one arm to encircle my waist, the other to hold the rock, so we didn't sink.

Reaching between us, I slipped the hard yearning of Sean into my velvet heat. As Sean pushed in, the friction made me pant his name and drag my nails across his back.

"I'm yours, Holly," Sean breathed in my ear. My teeth

found his shoulder. "I promise I will love you right," he grunted as he thrust into me. "To always support you," he moaned as he withdrew and then punctuated it with another thrust. "We will be happy, Holly. I promise, I won't let you down."

Closing my eyes, happiness flooded me at his words. Taking his face in my hands, I forced his pacific eyes to lock with mine. "No secrets, Sean. No lies, and no secrets. Absolute honesty. That's all I ask. No nasty surprises."

Sean groaned hard, his face dropped to my shoulder and his arm at my waist tightening as if he worried I'd slip away. "Always," he moaned. "As soon as we get back, I will tell you everything."

I clutched him to me in every way. "I love you," I confessed, my voice a mere breath by his ear.

Sean's entire body tensed. His next thrust was hard and deep. The sound of his groan was so primal it ripped into my core and demanded my body concede to my feelings for him. I threw my head back as my body exploded into a million stars of hot fiery pleasure.

Sean cursed and thrust harder and deeper, driving me further out of my body and out of my mind. "Jesus, Holly." Sean pushed me hard into the rock behind me. His teeth gripped my shoulder, then he yelled his ecstasy into my flesh as he claimed my body for him.

My eyes widened with shock. With Sean pulsing inside of me, I understood how intimate sex without protection was. That from this moment onwards, it would always mean so much more for me.

Sean lifted his face, his eyes glassy with pleasure and happiness. "I love you, Holly Claire."

"I love you too."

The sun was radiating joy as we made our way back to the resort. The ring on my finger sparkling in the sunlight, Sean's eyes much the same. We kept looking over at each other, smiling, and my cheeks would heat every time, which made Sean laugh.

As we walked back to the main resort, I noticed a bunch

of news vans parked out front. "What's going on?"

Sean's smile dropped a little. "An American senator is staying with us. There was some debacle yesterday on the mainland. He's holding a press conference today to give his opinion on how that will affect his state." As we approached the doors, Sean's steps slowed. "I'm going to duck in to check how it is going. How about you head home and shower."

Smiling, I went up on tiptoes to kiss him. It was a little more than appropriate for public, but it matched the intensity of my feelings.

Sean chuckled to himself when a valet wolf whistled. "I'll see you in an hour." Stepping inside, Sean collected some clothes from Henry to change. Possibly so he wasn't greeting the senator as the manager in a pair of boardshorts and shirt.

With a smile and no interest in politics, I started skipping to the side entrance to head back to the cottage. Passing by one of the news vans, the screen on the open side of it caught my attention. I stopped dead, confused as Raymond stood addressing the press.

Blinking rapidly, I approached the van. Inside a man was pressing buttons and adjusting volumes. He looked at me with a frown. "Mind if I watch a little?"

"That's fine. Here, you can listen as well. He pulled the cord of his headphones, and Raymond's voice filled the van. Raymond was discussing a shooting at a shopping center. Looking disgusted as he tallied the dead, Raymond shook his head. "America needs to learn from places like Australia. We need to look to countries which have introduced gun laws successfully. We need to take steps to protect our people against the modernism that our amendments were never written to consider..."

"Who is that?" My stomach was tensing.

"Senator Raymond Cassidy. He's the sitting rep for San Francisco, so the majority of his constituents support his stance on gun laws.

"How long has he been senator for?" I asked, my hands clenching my dress.

"About eight years now. Cassidy's a good man, but a typical lawyer and politician, if you know what I mean?"

I certainly did. Four days and not once did Raymond or Sean tell me he was in politics, and Sean knew how I felt about political families. My stomach dropped as Raymond called his conference about gun control to an end. He smiled calling Sean up on stage. Sean didn't look happy, but he took the spot beside his father.

"You all know my son, Sean. I've been trying to encourage him to run for office locally. When I told him, he should get into politics, he told me he'd think about it. I didn't expect him to take that to mean start dating the daughter of someone holding office."

My throat constricted, fists clenching the skirt of my dress. Sean's jaw clenching while the reporters laughed. "I am proud to say that Holly Claire, the daughter of Australian Prime Minister Nathan Claire, has agreed to marry my son."

"Are you okay?" The man in the van asked.

I couldn't unclench my fists to wipe the tears streaking down my cheeks. "Is this local?" I inquired, trying to hold myself together.

"No, it's national. Why?"

"When will it go to air?" I knew my father's cabinet monitored American politics closely. There is no way they would miss this.

"It's live."

I nearly screamed. So much so, I had to cover my mouth, the dress still clenched in my fist, to stop it coming out. When I resisted that urge, my next instinct was to vomit.

"Hey, you don't look well. Should I call someone?" The man asked turning the sound off so he could focus on me. Raymond was still talking, Sean standing there, playing the part of the perfect son. I knew that look. I'd played that part half my life, watched my brothers and sisters play it during my father's campaign. I hated it.

"I'm fine. I need to go." I was anything but fine. Pulling out my phone, I headed back to the cottage.

My father's people would be all over this in a matter of

minutes if it were live. The Australian people barely knew there was a third daughter; I doubt the Americans did. Raymond had made me a public figure just by putting my name in the same sentence as my father's. Australian tabloids would be all over this, digging up the old scandal. Every journalist would want to find the dirty details of my estrangement from my family.

Thirty minutes later, I was carrying my bag back to the front of the hotel when my phone started ringing again. Ignoring it, I stopped by the door and spoke to a taxi driver, giving him my bag before I stepped inside. Spotting Henry, I waved to get his attention.

"Miss Claire, I hear congratulations are in order?" Henry greeted.

Taking a deep breath so not to burst into tears, I held my emotions in check. "Do you know where Sean is, Henry? The taxi is waiting to take me to the airport."

Henry frowned. "I'll find him for you." Walking to the concierge desk, Henry picked up the phone. "Sean, its Henry. Holly is waiting at the front door for you." Taking a breath, Henry's eyes flicked over me. "Ah, to say goodbye. Her taxi is waiting." Henry looked at the phone surprised and hung it up. "Um, he's on his way."

"Thanks, Henry. Goodbye."

"Goodbye, Miss Claire. Have a safe travel home."

Stepping outside, I waited by the taxi. Sean came running out the door a minute later, just as my phone started ringing again. Checking it, I pressed the silent button. "What's going on?" Sean asked, worried. When his eyes met mine, his shoulders sagged. "Holly..."

My phone started ringing again. "My father's press secretary has tried to call me twenty times in twenty minutes." Pressing silent again, I felt the first tear escape. "Had I not watched your father's broadcast, I would have answered the first call. But I did. So, I know exactly what has his boxers wedged up his arse to have him calling for the first time in years."

Sean's face dropped. "Holly, I can explain."

Cassidy

"It's too late!" I met Sean's eyes. "I asked you straight out if there was anything I needed to know, anything that could be an issue for us. You didn't tell me."

"I know how you feel about father's in politics. You made that very clear, Holly. I was going to tell you in Molokai, but we got interrupted. I was going to tell you when we got back just now. It doesn't matter. What my father does shouldn't impact us," Sean argued angrily.

Henry and the valets raising brows as they pretended not to listen.

"I agree, it shouldn't have. Had you told me in Molokai that it could be an issue, I could have prepared myself for it." Silencing my phone again, I shook my head. "At the falls, when I asked for truth, you still had a chance. But the moment your father made me a public figure, by putting my name right beside my father's, it affected us."

"I didn't know he was going to do that," Sean pleaded.

"But you stood there and let him. You told him not to tell me he was a politician, right? Before I met him, you warned him, didn't you?" Sean bowed his head. "So, you deceived me on purpose."

"Holly, please? It was new and I didn't want you not to give us a chance because my father is a senator. How is it fair to judge me because of his career choice?"

"Jesus, Sean! Do you understand the media storm your dad caused for me? I'm not just the prime minister's daughter. I'm his estranged daughter. To a tabloid that spells family disgrace, or horrible family secret." I swiped at the angry emotions spilling down my face. "You should have told me about your dad, and you should have told your dad to keep me out of it."

Slipping the engagement ring off my finger, I put it in his hand. "I love you, Sean. I would have been faithful to you in every way. But, I will not stand in the background smiling and used for someone's political gain. That boat sailed years ago, and I'm not getting back on board ever again." Kissing his cheek, I turned to climb into the taxi.

"No!" Sean growled, grabbing my wrist, his eyes pleading

as he turned me to face him. "You promised to come back."

"You lied to me. Even when we came back, you still didn't tell me this was about your father."

My phone started ringing a different tone. This time my father's face flashed on the screen above DAD. Sean watched the screen as I pressed the decline button.

"I'm sorry, Holly. I wanted to tell you. But, I knew how you felt about these things, about the way your father judges you because of your boyfriends. I didn't want to lose you over something irrelevant." My phone went off again. Sean took it from my hand and turned it off before handing it back to me. "Stay. Let me protect you from this?"

Irate and struggling to stay calm, I was beyond angry that one sentence could turn my life upside down. "God, you should have told me. Even this morning, it would have changed everything right now. But you deceived me, Sean. How do I trust you again now?"

"I will never lie to you, Holly. My father was the only thing I've kept from you?"

"I never lied at all." Stepping into Sean, I kissed his lips lightly. "I wanted you to be different." Stepping towards the taxi again, I found those steps the hardest I'd ever taken in my life. "I have to go. I moved my flight forward. Goodbye, Sean."

CHAPTER EIGHTEEN

Arriving home was a sweet relief, and a painful acceptance. Sean let me leave. He didn't turn up at the airport and sweep me off my feet with a passionate kiss and promises never to break my heart again. My life wasn't a movie; it was cold harsh reality.

Stopping at the phone store on the way home, I told them I needed a new unlisted number. Explaining to the salesman I was receiving harassing phone calls got me very fast service.

Messaging Trisha, Mitch and Roger the number, I told them I was home. Collapsing on my lounge, I contemplated checking the news.

Eventually, I unpacked my bags and settled for crying into my pillow. "So, I guess we're not moving to Hawaii?" Trisha queried at the door.

"Aren't you meant to be at work?"

"Yeah, but then I saw on the news. Something about the Prime Minister's estranged daughter getting engaged. Then your message arrived with a new number, and I kinda figured shit might have gone down. So, I developed a stomach bug." Trisha kicked off her work shoes and came to sit on my bed. "What happened, Holly?"

Giving Trisha the summary, she huffed and collapsed on the bed next to me. "He should have told you. That's a huge deal considering your past. Did he know?"

"Yes."

"Then he fucked up, and he needs to own that." We lay there staring at the ceiling for several minutes before Trisha sighed. "He better get on a plane and chase after you?"

"If he doesn't?"

"Then it wasn't true love."

There was loud knocking at the door. We both sat up and looked at each other. No one ever knocked on our door like that. A moment later there was a crashing sound out on my balcony.

"What the hell?" Jumping to my feet as loud cursing came from the balcony. Pulling back my blind, I found Mitchell trying to right the pot plants he'd knocked over.

"Holly, there are some serious looking dudes at your door. Did you blow something up?" Mitchell whispered. "Don't answer that. Here, I'll throw you onto my balcony, and you can hide next door till they are gone."

Groaning, I opened the sliding door. "Not necessary. I'm not under arrest." Turning back to Trisha, I huffed. "This is going to get ugly."

"I'll brew the coffee. You get changed. You can't stand up for yourself with a tear streaked face and pussycat pajamas."

"I'll help with the coffee." Mitchell hugged me on the way through my room. "There is a tone of reporters downstairs too."

"Argh, we are going to have to move," I complained.

After changing, and many more bangs at the door telling me they knew I was home, I opened the door to my father. Well, his bodyguard's chest. His security came in first and ensured no potential assassins lay in wait. Why they discounted me, was beyond me, but they asked Mitchell and Trisha to leave.

"Get stuffed! This is my house and my friend. I'm not leaving her alone in a room full of strange armed men." Trisha tapped her toe.

"I'm her father." Dad rolled his eyes.

"As I said," Trisha shrugged. Picking up her coffee, Trisha sat her curvy behind on the couch. I tried very hard not to laugh.

My father glared daggers at us. "It's okay. I doubt she's dangerous," Dad dismissed his security. Waiting till the door closed, he removed his jacket. "Don't I get a hug?"

"No. What do you want?"

Dad cleared his throat. "I hear congratulations are in order?"

"Oh, you heard about my new job? Thanks, yes, I'm very excited," I smiled leaning against the kitchen counter. "Didn't think you would be interested."

"I meant your engagement."

Frowning, I looked at Trisha, she shrugged, I looked back to my father and picked up my coffee. "No idea what you are talking about, Nathan, or is it Mr. Prime Minister?"

"Dad still works."

"Never has before. Anyway, I'm single like always, so I don't know what poor information you've received." I took a mouthful of my coffee.

"U.S. Senator Cassidy announced you were engaged to his son only twenty-four hours ago in Hawaii. A country I happen to know you only arrived back from this morning," Dad argued.

"Would you like some coffee?" I offered.

"No, thank you. I would like a straight answer."

"Are you sure, because Trisha makes the best coffee."

"I'm sure. Are you engaged to Sean Cassidy?"

"It's the best coffee in the Southern Hemisphere. You're missing out."

"Forget the damn coffee, are you engaged?" Nathan finally yelled.

The room went silent. I glared at my father. "No. When I realized he was a senator's son, I remembered my experience dating a prime minister's son. I decided not to repeat history."

"You broke up with him?"

"Yes."

"Because his father is a senator?"

"Because his father didn't announce his son's engagement to me. He announced Sean's engagement to your daughter! It shouldn't have mattered who my father was. But, in this case, considering the nature of our relationship..."

Nathan studied his polished shoes. "Were you in love with him?"

"What does it matter, Nathan? You don't care, you never have. Your interest has always been the same as Raymond Cassidy's. 'What does that connection gain you?' Well, there is no connection anymore, so if that's all you are here for, there is the door."

Dad took a deep breath, counting to ten under his breath. "What is your new job?"

"I'm the general manager of a hotel," I answered with only half the pride I felt.

"You finally got your dream job? Well, done. It's good to know that screwing your boss got you somewhere."

My coffee mug smashed against the wall beside him. "Get the fuck out!" I yelled at him. Trisha was beside me pulling me towards my bedroom as security burst in to see what the hell happened.

"Get out and never come back. I hate you! Get out!" I screamed at him. "You're a shit dad. Do you know that? That's why you have a son with a drug problem, a porn star daughter, and another who doesn't want anything to do with you. Because you're an asshole and you don't deserve a minute of my time. Now, get out!"

"Come on, Holly. Go take a breather." Trisha shoved me into my room and shut the door. "Seriously?!" She scolded my father. "The girl's heartbroken because she's a blood relation to you, and all you can do is criticize her. I agree, get out. She's too good to be your daughter. Was she adopted?"

"I've never understood that girl. She gives up the men in her life for the most illogical reasons."

"Freud says it all comes back to the parents. Maybe take a look in the mirror and figure out why you caused your daughter to give up the love of her life?"

"I'll show myself out."

"You can't help yourself, can you? The new job, had nothing to do with her ex. She got it because she's that good at her job. If you knew anything about her, you'd know that,"

Trisha responded. "I can't believe Holly's related to you because she's actually got a heart."

The door closed. Trisha exhaled hard. "Okay, honey. Daddy jerkyl has left the building."

Sighing, I got control of my emotions. "I'm sorry about the coffee mug."

Opening the door, Trisha dropped onto my bed next to me. "Forget the mug. That was bloody good coffee you wasted on that arse."

"Sorry."

Putting her arm around me, Trisha rested her head against mine. "What happens now, Holly?"

"Life."

~To be continued …~

About the Author

Ebony lives in Sydney, Australia, with her husband, daughter, and six cats. She loves to read fantasy, thrillers, and paranormal romance, spending most of her free time with her nose in a book or writing.

Having always possessed an over-active imagination she spent her younger years regaling friends with fantastic stories, holding her audience captive with the passion and suspense of her characters plights.

Now in adulthood she has numerous published works and shows no signs of stopping her imagination from spreading across as many pages as it can find.

If you'd like to follow Ebony or simply say hi you can find her here:

Facebook: www.facebook.com/EbonyOlson.Author/
Dedicated Hotel Series Fan Page:
https://www.facebook.com/groups/330072697715454

Twitter: @Ebony_Olson

Website: http://ebonyolson.com/